"I want to order some flowers," Adam announced conspiratorially

As he stood inches away from Diane in the back room of her shop, she could smell his warm, musky scent.

"What did you have in mind?" she asked, trying to ignore the feelings he aroused in her.

"Something romantic," he said in a husky tone. "Something that will really impress the woman I'm sending them to."

Diane's heart sank. He'd met someone. They hadn't even had two dates together and now . . .

"Of course, I'll need a card, too," he added with a spark of mischief in his eyes. *Damn him.* "Maybe you could write the address for me."

"How would I know the address?" Diane asked, outrage in her voice.

"Don't you know where you live?" he murmured, as he came closer. "The flowers are for you," he continued, pulling her to him.

"For me?" she asked. "A goodbye bouquet?"

His gaze dropped to her mouth, making her quiver with anticipation. "Lady, this is as far from a goodbye bouquet as you'll ever get." When his mouth closed in on hers, Diane knew Adam's words were for real. . . .

Pamela Roth's second Temptation romance tackles in a witty, upbeat way one of the hottest issues of the 1990s—how to avoid being caught in the fast-track race and enjoy life. Also known as Pamela Toth, Pam is an established romance author. She lives near Seattle with her entire family—including dog, Siamese cats and numerous tropical fish—or, as her daughter once put it, a "whole food chain!"

Books by Pamela Roth

HARLEQUIN TEMPTATION
254–TOO MANY WEDDINGS

Easy Does It

PAMELA ROTH

Harlequin Books

TORONTO • NEW YORK • LONDON
AMSTERDAM • PARIS • SYDNEY • HAMBURG
STOCKHOLM • ATHENS • TOKYO • MILAN

This book is dedicated to Bonnie Drury, good friend and
fellow writer whose letters always brighten my day

Published August 1991

ISBN 0-373-25459-8

EASY DOES IT

Printed in U.S.A.

1

ADAM WESTOVER STUDIED the woman seated across from him and wondered why he wasn't more upset that she'd put an end to their affair. Sheila was pretty and bright, she had a wicked sense of humor and a figure that made men walk into walls. Over the last two months, Adam had enjoyed dating her.

Still, there was something missing in their relationship. He knew it and obviously Sheila did, too. That was probably why she had managed to get seriously involved with another man without Adam even noticing.

"Jason's really wonderful," Sheila said with a dreamy sigh as she drank the last of her wine. "I know you'd like him."

Adam squeezed her hand reassuringly. "I know I would," he agreed, not having the slightest interest in ever meeting the other man. "And I'm really happy for you."

That much was true. Adam *was* happy for her. And just the tiniest bit envious. From the glow to Sheila's cheeks and the light in her eyes, it was easy to see she was in love. Adam was beginning to envy anyone who could feel that much emotion. Then he remembered that the kind of love Sheila described wasn't for him. He'd had his chance. And blown it.

"You're taking this so well," she said, a tiny frown appearing between her beautifully arched brows as she pushed back her chair. "I thought you'd be more upset."

Adam got up. He never allowed himself to care enough to be jealous, let alone get hurt. He didn't dare; instead he had casual relationships that ended civilly, turning into casual friendships. It was safer for everyone involved.

He managed to smile as he stood and held her chair, then glanced at the check. Tossing some bills onto the table, he escorted Sheila from the small bar where she'd asked him to meet her. Outside, she turned to face him.

"Well," she said briskly, "I'm glad we're still friends, and I'm sure we'll see each other around." Her hand lifted to touch his cheek. "'Bye."

Adam touched her arm. "Take care," he said, watching her as she walked to her car and drove away. Feeling oddly depressed, he crossed the street to where his own '55 Chev convertible was parked. The engine purred quietly when he started it. On the way home, he idly stroked the leather seat cover as he thought about what his sister had told him only the week before.

"One day," Lori had said earnestly, "you'll meet the right woman. Things will work out this time, you'll see. Just don't give up on love." She had twisted her engagement ring around and around on her slim finger, giving him a smile that was meant to be encouraging. "I mean it, Adam. Quit blaming yourself for what happened to Penny. You'll find someone else."

He wasn't at all sure that he wanted to find someone else. Having failed his wife when she needed him the most, perhaps he didn't deserve another chance.

Adam pulled into the garage behind his apartment. He lived in a small but attractive complex on a quiet side street in the northern California town that had been his home for several years. He shut off the motor and reactivated the automatic garage door control. Then he sat for a moment in the dimness, staring at nothing, running a hand through his dark hair.

He had everything he needed—a business he loved, friends, a comfortable life-style. So why was he parked in his garage in the near dark of early evening, speculating about what was missing? Why didn't he just sit back and enjoy the life he had put together for himself?

Had it been when Lori had announced her engagement to his best friend, Tom Braddock, that a certain restless longing had begun to nag at him? All it took to effectively squelch those feelings and strengthen his resolve was for him to replay certain memories. Commitment wasn't for him. He had made that decision and he meant to stick with it.

It was just that sometimes, like tonight when the air was warm and scented, when the day was mellowing into darkness, that a sense of isolation gripped him. But only temporarily. Setting his jaw, Adam got out of the car, shutting the garage door behind him.

DIANE SIMMONS SAT behind a battered desk in the back of her florist shop writing out checks. The bell over the front door tinkled loudly, signaling the arrival of a customer. Remembering that today was Carol's day off, Diane grumbled under her breath as she stuck her pen behind her ear and pushed open the door to the showroom.

The man waiting at the counter was dark-haired and exceptionally tall. Diane usually didn't allow herself the time to notice if a man was handsome, but this one's long muscular body in T-shirt and snug jeans caught and held her attention. He was the perfect height for her own five feet, nine inches. Somewhere in his thirties, she would guess as he turned and smiled. And probably married. Buying flowers for his wife.

The man's eyes, beneath thick straight brows, were framed with a fringe of dark lashes. Brown eyes, she noticed. A smile curved his mouth enticingly above his strong chin. Diane did her best to ignore the reaction that shivered through her.

"How can I help you?" She answered the easy grin with a professional one of her own. She hadn't seen this man before and was always on the lookout for new customers.

"I need something nice," he said. His voice was deep, slowed to a drawl. "A goodbye bouquet."

Diane stopped. "Beg your pardon?" Had she heard him right?

"You know," the man said. "The kind of thing you send when you're no longer dating someone. Sort of a 'thanks and good luck.'"

Diane felt her smile fading. Without warning a picture of the yellow roses Earl had sent when he dumped her flashed into her mind.

"How much would you like to spend?" Diane's tone was distinctly unfriendly, and she hastily cleared her throat. This was a customer, she reminded herself. Be nice. Even if he was an unfeeling jerk, his money was as real as anyone else's.

Diane managed to pull her lips back into a smile of sorts. "I mean, if you would give me an idea of the price range you had in mind, I could suggest what kind of flowers might be appropriate." Skunk cabbage, she thought.

The man shrugged, glancing down the apron that covered most of her front. He mentioned a generous sum.

"You could get roses, a large mixed arrangement, or a nice potted plant." Diane showed him some bouquets in the cooler, and two azalea bushes in foil-covered pots. After a moment, he decided on yellow roses and baby's breath. Gritting her teeth, Diane took down the order and gave him an enclosure card to fill out.

"Do you want this sent tomorrow?" she asked.

Adam looked up at the woman standing behind the counter. "Sure. Tomorrow's fine. There's no hurry."

When he smiled and shrugged again, her eyes, so blue they were almost purple, seemed to get even darker, and her chin came up. He wondered if yellow roses stood for something he wasn't aware of. No matter, they were pretty, and he knew that Sheila liked roses.

"Of course there's no hurry," the woman muttered, pushing sun-streaked blond bangs off her forehead as she bent over the order form.

"Pardon me?" Adam wasn't sure he had heard right.

She glanced back up. "Nothing," she said. "I guess there wouldn't be any rush on a 'goodbye' bouquet, as you called it." She looked as if she was going to say more. Adam waited, but she didn't.

"It was just a casual relationship," he found himself elaborating. "You know."

The woman before him remained silent as she looked up at him with those amazing violet eyes, her cheeks gone pink. "This is an expensive farewell for a casual relationship," she commented.

"Well, it wasn't that casual, I guess. We did date for several months. But I was never serious about her."

Adam wasn't sure why he was trying to explain, but he could almost feel the woman's disapproval.

Her eyes narrowed at his words, and she seemed to be biting her lip. "Oh, I'm sure I understand *exactly* what you mean," she said. Her tone was definitely chilly.

Adam realized that she'd misunderstood him completely. The way he'd put it sounded awful. It shouldn't matter, but there was something about the way her eyes tilted up at the corners that he found fascinating. Her hair was streaked with sunlight and the color looked natural. Everything about her seemed natural—from the clear glow of her skin to the short, neatly trimmed nails on her long fingers. Ringless fingers, he was pleased to notice.

She was pretty, tall for a woman, but slim as near as he could tell with that white apron covering most of her. Still, he didn't need to justify himself. She probably couldn't care less anyway.

"I always send a bouquet," Adam added despite himself. Why hadn't he come in here before? "It seems a nice way to end things."

The polite smile on her mouth froze in place. "I'm sure," she said. "If you always send flowers, you would want to do it this time, too. Even if the recipient didn't mean a thing to you."

Put that way, his intentions sounded even worse than they were. Had she emphasized the word "always" just a little? Adam winced at the icy look in her eyes, sure now that if he hadn't been a customer, she would have said more. As it was, she seemed to be having trouble restraining herself.

He stuck out his hand, intending to distract her. "By the way, my name's Adam Westover."

She hesitated, staring at his outstretched hand before sliding hers into it. "Diane Simmons." Her grip was firm, fingers toughened by work.

"You must be the owner." What an inane comment, considering the sign—Diane's Flowers—over the front door! He could usually do better than that, but there was something about Diane Simmons that threw him. It had to be her disapproval. Adam wasn't used to that faintly condemning expression.

"Yes, I'm the owner. If you're finished with the card . . ." Her tone hovered between polite and chilly.

Adam glanced down at what he had written. *Good luck. Your friend, Adam.* He knew that Sheila would see the humor in that. She had said they would stay friends. His gaze rose, colliding with Diane's. For an uncomfortable moment he wondered if she could read upside down.

Diane was having a difficult time keeping herself from looking at what Adam had written. She was burning with curiosity, wondering if he had already broken up with the woman or if this bouquet and small card were meant to do the dirty work for him as roses had for Earl, who hadn't bothered to tell her in person that their affair was over. She was tempted to fill Adam Westover's order with dead flowers.

No, that wouldn't be fair. Or professional. It wasn't Adam's girlfriend's fault that he was a jerk. The poor woman deserved a beautiful bouquet, the prettiest Diane could provide. Perhaps it would be some small consolation.

Diane glanced at the address on the check Adam handed her, then at the driver's license he held out.

"It's okay," she said. "You're local, so I don't need your ID."

Adam Westover was printed on the check, a nice masculine name. It suited his lean handsome face, his tall broad-shouldered body. Diane gave herself a mental shake. The man was a heartless womanizer. Hadn't he said he "always" sent bouquets?

"Anything else you need?" His voice cut through her thoughts like flowing honey. Smooth.

Diane looked into his eyes. There were shadows in their depths. That surprised her.

"We'll take care of this tomorrow, first thing," Diane replied, stretching her lips again. Maybe *he* didn't care when the woman got her flowers, but Diane did. She handed him his copy of the order. "Maybe you'd like to open an account. That way you could just phone in your orders."

His dark eyes narrowed. "I don't know if it would be worth the bother," he said. "I don't buy that many flowers."

"I could put you on our mailing list, too," Diane offered, ignoring his comment. "For special sales and things like that."

"Not just now." Something in his tone warned her not to push him too far.

"Whatever is best for you," she told him in a sweet tone.

"Right." Adam pushed his wallet into the back pocket of his worn jeans. Diane did her best not to notice how the motion pulled the fabric tight across his hips.

Then he hesitated, as if he wanted to add something.

"Yes?" Diane didn't care anymore that her voice was less than friendly. As badly as she needed business, as many bouquets as a man like this might buy, she told herself she didn't need *his* business.

"My shop is one street over," Adam said, pointing. "Custom Car Design. Perhaps you've seen it?"

Diane had noticed the building and the beautifully painted automobiles that were sometimes parked out front. She had dreamed of a new paint job for her ancient wagon, but it wasn't in her budget.

"I'm afraid not. I don't go down that street."

Adam's smile faded. "Oh. Well, if you ever want to, come by and I'll give you the tour."

"I'm pretty busy right here," Diane said.

"Sure, I understand. We'll probably see each other around, then. I'm surprised we never met before."

Diane didn't respond.

Adam glanced back as he turned toward the door. "You have a nice place here. I know you haven't been open long, and I wish you luck with your business."

"Thank you," Diane said grudgingly.

He seemed reluctant to leave. "It's just that I know how hard it is to get started," he said. "If things seem tough sometimes..." His voice trailed off as she merely stared.

"Well," Adam said, "don't give up, that's all I meant."

Diane almost smiled, a real smile, only schooling her lips at the last minute. For a moment there he had looked unsure, hesitant. It was probably an expression he had worked on, and it was undoubtedly effective. But not on her.

Squaring her shoulders and flipping the order book shut, Diane glanced toward the door to the back room as if something urgent waited for her there.

Finally Adam touched his fingers to his forehead in a casual salute. "See you."

"Goodbye," Diane said formally, going into the office before he was even out the front door. She was feeling distinctly grumpy from her confrontation with him and, to her surprise, slightly winded. As if she had been running. Or holding her breath. She stabbed her copy of his order onto the spindle with more force than was necessary and dropped back into the scarred steno chair, banishing Adam Westover and his love life from her mind.

Walking back to his own shop, Adam thought that it wasn't often that he made such a hash of things as he had with the blonde at Diane's Flowers. She had admitted to being the owner but she hadn't been very responsive when he wished her luck with the business. Perhaps she was doing so well that she didn't need his good wishes, but he always felt a certain kinship with other businessmen in the neighborhood. Businesspersons, he amended.

With that silky blond hair and those violet eyes, the florist reminded him more of Diana the Huntress than Diane the shop owner. Picturing her in a short, clinging toga, bow and arrows gripped in one hand, Adam almost laughed out loud. He was really getting fanciful.

It was clear she hadn't been impressed by *him*, not by a long shot. No point in thinking about her.

ADAM'S SISTER'S wedding was the next weekend and he still hadn't bought her a present. Or gotten a haircut or polished the shoes he was wearing with his rented tux. While he took care of those things, Adam had to keep reminding himself he had decided not to think about Diane Simmons. Besides, even though her hands were bare, she still might be married or otherwise involved.

Not that it mattered. Involvement didn't interest him. Not hers, and definitely not his own.

The day of the wedding dawned warm and sunny, the sky so blue it looked artificial. Adam was busy that morning calming down the groom and picking up the tuxedos, calling his sister with some last-minute advice. He scarcely had time to think, especially about cool blondes who ran flower shops.

After starting a few minutes late, the ceremony went off without a hitch. Adam heard the emotion in Tom's voice when he said his vows, and saw the happy tears that shimmered in Lori's eyes. His own eyes filled as he watched his little sister and his best friend exchange their first kiss as husband and wife. Happiness surrounded them like a golden halo.

DIANE REALLY HAD intended to be well away from the reception hall before any of the guests got there, but she'd been caught in a traffic jam and had arrived late. She took no chances with her jobs, giving each one her personal attention. Satisfied customers would make her business grow; she hoped the wedding guests would notice the flowers and remember where they came from.

She was still setting out the tree roses on either side of the bandstand when the members of the wedding party came in the main doors, followed by a stream of guests. Luckily Diane had already placed the centerpieces on each table and only had a few more flowers left to put around the room's perimeter.

She was repositioning the last pot of azaleas when the bride and groom came over in their wedding finery. Tom's tuxedo was dark blue, his fair coloring a contrast to his bride's dark hair and brown eyes. Lori looked like a fairy princess in her white gown, bodice embroidered with pearls and full skirt billowing almost to the floor. An elaborate coronet trimmed with more pearls held back a frothy veil.

"Thank you for the terrific job you did with the flowers," Lori told Diane.

"We'll recommend you to all our friends," her new husband added with a smile.

"Thank you, and congratulations," Diane said. "But now I'd better be going." She was dressed for work in a neat but ordinary blouse and skirt with comfortable, flat-heeled sandals, hair skinned back into a ponytail, lip gloss nibbled off. Next to the bride she felt like Cinderella before the fairy godmother's arrival.

Tom gazed down at Lori with an expression that made Diane's breath catch. Feeling like an intruder, she started to turn away.

"Oh, please don't leave," Lori exclaimed. "Have something to eat first."

Diane glanced down self-consciously. "Thanks, but I'm not really dressed for this."

"We insist," the groom said firmly. "Please stay. At least have a glass of champagne and something from the buffet. I saw you working at the church earlier. You must be hungry."

Before Diane could deny it, her stomach chose that moment to rumble loudly. All three of them laughed.

"Thanks," she said. "I guess I will."

"Good." The bride turned from Diane to her groom. "Back to our duties." She gave him a warm smile. Again Diane felt like an intruder as she saw the love reflected on their faces. She watched them with a trace of envy as they walked, hands linked, toward the entrance to the hall, where the receiving line was forming.

Diane was intent on grabbing a bite and getting out of there. The kind of love the newlyweds shared might make her sigh, but she didn't have time for love right now. She had a business to run.

In the receiving line, Adam shifted to make room for his sister and her brand-new husband. He had noticed Diane Simmons the moment he walked into the hall, and only duty kept him from approaching her.

Beside him, Lori squeezed his arm. "I did what you asked," she said. "But the rest is up to you. And don't forget that I want an explanation later."

Adam thanked her absently as he watched Diane, his expression thoughtful. Had she noticed him yet? Did she remember him?

Diane chose the most unobtrusive table to sit at and eat the finger food she'd taken from the buffet and sip with gratitude a cup of black coffee. It wouldn't have been polite to ignore the wedding couple's thoughtful offer, but she did have to get back to the shop. Saturdays were always busy. Lori waved from her place in the receiving line as Diane sat down, glad she'd taken the time to do as they suggested.

Idly she let her gaze drift, until her progress was halted abruptly by the sight of a familiar figure.

Adam Westover! What was he doing there? And looking even more attractive than she remembered.

Of course. Same last name as the bride; Diane hadn't thought. She debated leaving, but suddenly the food on her plate was too great a temptation—or was it the prospect of meeting Adam again that kept her seated?

She had finished the last of her canapés as some of the members of the wedding party began to drift toward the food, leaving the bride, groom and both sets of parents surrounded by a knot of guests. On the stage a band was playing softly. As Diane watched them, draining her coffee cup, the chair next to hers was abruptly dragged back.

"Mind if I join you?"

She tensed at the resonant voice and looked up. Adam, stunning in his dark tuxedo, was holding a loaded plate in one hand and two tall glasses of champagne in the other. Diane glanced around but he appeared to be alone.

"Sit here if you like," she said, feeling like a frump next to his elegant finery. "I was just leaving."

Before Diane could rise, Adam put down the plate and the two glasses, sloshing a few drops of champagne. "What a coincidence to see you here. Let's drink a toast before you go," he suggested.

Diane narrowed her eyes and braced herself against her troubling response to his nearness. "Why?"

Her blunt question obviously surprised him, but Adam recovered with a wicked grin. "Because my sister's happier than I've ever seen her," he said. "Because she married a guy I think will keep her happy."

Diane's knees wobbled dangerously in reaction to his smile. "So Lori is your sister," she said inanely, then bit her lip. The last thing she wanted was to make conversation with the goodbye bouquet man.

"That's right." He hesitated, as if weighing his words carefully. "I haven't been able to get you out of my mind since I ordered those flowers."

Diane swallowed, stunned. "You're outrageous," she croaked.

If anything, Adam's grin widened as he sat down beside her. "Sometimes I am," he agreed, leaning closer and placing a champagne glass in her hand. "I can also be amusing, serious, or touchingly humble." He bowed his head briefly as he uttered the last words. Then he clinked his glass to hers. "To us."

He sampled the champagne as Diane watched it ripple down his throat, wondering just when she had lost control of the situation. She wasn't sure if Adam Westover was conceited or crazy, but she almost wished she had the time to find out.

As she sipped her champagne, there was a drumroll and the bandleader announced that the bride and groom were about to begin the dancing. Diane joined in the applause as Tom led Lori onto the floor. He opened his arms and she floated into them as the music swelled, the song unabashedly romantic. A sigh escaped Diane's lips as she watched the couple gliding across the floor. They looked so happy.

After a few slow turns, the groom signaled for other couples to join them. Diane pushed back her chair, hoping to escape without fuss. But when Adam stood beside her and held out his hand, she realized she didn't have a chance.

"Dance?" he asked, devilishly handsome in his formal wear, dark eyes twinkling. "Please?" he added when she didn't immediately reply.

Diane shook her head. "I'm not a guest," she said. "Technically, I'm working."

Adam crowded close. "I won't tell if you don't." His breath teased her cheek. "Besides, aren't you the boss?"

"More reason than ever for me not to goof off. And I'm not dressed for it."

Adam glanced at her clothes. "I'd say you're the best-looking woman here," he said when his attention had returned to her face. "You're just fine the way you are."

Diane could feel the heat of embarrassment climb her neck and spill onto her cheeks. She wasn't used to compliments unless they pertained to her flowers. She had been too busy over the last few years saving money to take the time for relationships, with one disastrous exception. Even with Earl she had been too busy to notice they were drifting apart until it was way too late. Perhaps he had been just the slightest bit justified in breaking it off, but even so he could have done it with more sensitivity than by sending those roses and the terse note.

"No," Diane told Adam again. "I couldn't possibly go on the dance floor now. I have to leave."

He glanced down at her empty plate and coffee cup, and his brows rose questioningly. "Lunch break over?" he asked.

"That was your sister's idea. It would have been rude to refuse." Her voice sounded defensive, even to her own ears.

"Humor me," he said, tugging gently at her arm. "One dance, and I promise I'll let you get back to work. And we won't tell your boss. She sounds like a slave driver."

He was standing so close that Diane was again aware of his scent, a combination of pine mixed with his own clean male fragrance. Some part of her was pleased that he didn't favor the more intense masculine colognes; part of her wished there was *something* about him she didn't find attractive.

There was heat, too, between them. She felt herself weakening. What could one dance hurt?

2

THE FLOOR WAS CROWDED when Diane glanced that way, the other dancers much too preoccupied to wonder for more than a moment about her casual attire. She wished she had taken the time for lipstick and had combed her hair out loose. Recognizing the direction of her thoughts, she gave herself a mental shake. Dancing with the brother of a customer when the work was done was one thing. Taking time away from the business to pretty herself up for some man was a different pot of posies altogether. Perhaps she had better take him up on that dance, then she could get her mind back to the really important things in her life.

Besides, Adam didn't look as if he was going anywhere until she gave in.

"Okay," she said, obviously surprising him. "One dance."

The lightning flash of his smile was ample reward. He slipped an arm around her waist and escorted her to the crowded floor as if she were visiting royalty, while Diane did her best to ignore the warmth that radiated from his body. Lori and her husband swept by in a glow of happiness, and she waved at Diane over his broad shoulder.

Diane smiled back. The music was sweetly seductive— Adam's arms were a haven of masculine strength. After a moment of moving together at a distance, he pulled her closer, snaking both arms around her waist. Diane hesitated, then curled her hands into the thick hair at his nape, putting aside her responsibilities long enough to lean into him and savor the sweet sensation of being free from anything more complex than following his lead.

"Wasn't this a good idea?" he asked. His voice sounded different, almost urgent.

Diane forced herself to meet his intense gaze. "Yes, it was." There was no point in denying what her body was responding to so readily. Adam's height, the breadth of his shoulders, his wiry frame all contributed to the sense of perfection that surrounded her like a hazy cloud. He was graceful for a tall man, guiding her easily around the floor. She was really beginning to enjoy herself when the number came to an end.

"One more," Adam said, and it wasn't a question.

Diane nodded, her attention settling at his bow tie. If he looked into her eyes, what might they reveal to him? She screened them with her lashes as the music began again. What harm in a few more moments of freedom? A tiny voice inside whispered to her that the harm had already been done, but Diane ignored it.

When the song ended, Adam's arm shifted reluctantly. He knew better than to push his luck, but he hated to let her go.

"How about lunch sometime next week?" he asked, keeping his voice casual as they left the floor.

"Sorry," Diane said immediately, not even taking the time to consider the request. "I grab a sandwich at the shop." She eyed him almost accusingly. "Do you take a real lunch hour?"

Her question surprised him. He'd never really thought about it—locking the door on his current project and flipping a sign in the window that said he'd be gone for an hour. Anyone who really wanted to talk to him would come back.

"I hope I'm never so busy I can't leave when I want to," he said as Diane stopped and turned toward him.

For a moment her intriguing eyes searched his. "We have very different ideas of success." Her tone was slightly censorious, and Adam bristled.

"I don't want to sell my soul into slavery," he said lightly, remembering the past and what it had cost.

After a moment of stunned silence, Diane laughed as he stood there feeling foolish. "I knew there were basic differences between us. Now I understand better what some of them are." She began to move away from him. "Thanks for the dance," she said, glancing back.

Adam watched her stop to exchange a word with his sister, then walk purposefully toward the exit. He had not only failed to impress her but had managed to totally condemn himself in her eyes. The feeling stayed with him as he spent the next hour circulating, dancing with preadolescent cousins who blushed and beamed at his attention, and elderly aunts who patted his cheek and told him he was a nice young man. Somehow he knew there was one female in town who probably wouldn't have agreed.

"LORI, ARE YOU in there?" Adam knocked again on the door to the room where he thought his sister was changing clothes.

"Just a minute," called a familiar voice.

Before Adam could say anything else, Lori's maid of honor, Cindy, opened the door, barring Adam's view. "She's half-dressed." The girl's tone was disapproving, but her eyes danced merrily.

"I've seen her half-dressed before," Adam said. "Remember, I'm her brother."

"Let him in," Lori said from the center of the room where she stood in a peach blouse and a cream slip. "I'm decent."

Adam slipped past Cindy, then glanced back at her. "Could I have a few minutes?"

"Sure. I'm going to grab another glass of champagne." She shut the door quietly behind her.

Lori stepped into her skirt, zipping it up. "You aren't going to talk to me about the birds and the bees, are you?"

Adam shoved his hands into his pants pockets. "I figured Mom already took care of that." A sudden flood of affection made him feel awkward. He and Lori had always had an easy relationship, filled with teasing, arguments and sticking up for each other. The emotion had been underlying but unspoken.

"You know I love you," Adam said bluntly.

Lori had been looking at her reflection in the full-length mirror. At his words, she turned. Her eyes, so like his own, filled with tears. Without a word, she came into his arms.

For a moment he just held her tight. Then she sniffed noisily and he stepped back and pulled out his handkerchief. "Don't cry. Tom will think I've been beating you, and I'd hate to have him mad at me."

Adam's teasing words made her smile through her tears. "You turkey," she said as he carefully blotted her cheeks. "I told myself I wouldn't cry, but things will always be different now, won't they?"

Adam put away the damp handkerchief and squeezed her shoulder. She was so slim and fragile; she looked so young. To him she would always be his baby sister. "Different, and better. I hope you're always as happy as you are today."

"With Tom, I will be," she said quietly. "And someday I want that happiness for you, too."

Adam shrugged, suddenly uncomfortable with the direction of their conversation. "Don't worry about me, okay? You concentrate on that husband of yours."

Lori touched his cheek. "I love you, too, you know."

Before Adam could reply, a knock sounded at the door and then their mother poked her head in. "Hello, dear," she said to Adam. "You'd better go so Lori can finish dressing."

Adam bent to kiss Lori's cheek. "I'll see you when you get back." When he let himself out, he heard her voice behind him. "Where's my other shoe?"

"NEED ANYTHING?" Adam opened the door a crack and called to Tom, who had gone to change from his tuxedo into more casual clothes.

"Come on in." Tom was buttoning a striped shirt he wore with cotton pants and white running shoes. "I'm glad to get out of that monkey suit. Do you think everyone's having a good time?"

"Yeah," Adam said, propping one shoulder against the wall. "And the ceremony went well."

Tom's grin widened. "Personally, I'm glad it's over. Now comes the best part."

"The weather in Mexico?" Adam asked innocently.

"The honeymoon!" Tom buckled his belt and turned to the mirror to comb his hair. "I know she's your kid sister," he said, "but she is one terrific woman."

Adam watched his friend's reflection. "You really love her," he said quietly.

Tom's eyes met his. "Yeah, I really love her." He turned. "Don't worry, I'll take good care of Lori." He stuck out his hand.

Adam gripped it firmly. "I know that."

For a moment the silence was charged with emotion—the unspoken affection between two close friends. Then Tom swiveled back to the mirror and took one last swipe at his blond hair. "It's about time you got interested in someone," he mumbled. "Ever since Penny died, you haven't let yourself get involved."

Adam straightened, reining in the sudden emotions that threatened to burst free. It had been two years since his wife died, and he still felt responsible.

"I've dated plenty of women," he said in a cool voice. "Just because I haven't told you—"

"Doesn't count," Tom interrupted, throwing things into a small duffel bag. "I'm talking involvement."

"You want me to get 'involved' with someone, to show you that I can?" Adam began defensively.

Tom reached out a hand to detain him as he pulled away. "No, man. I just think it's time you quit blaming yourself. Penny made her own choices. So you were trying to build a business and didn't have time to baby-sit her—"

Adam's hands balled into fists. "I should have been there for her," he blazed. "I knew she was dependent, easily led." He took a deep breath, reaching for calm. "If I hadn't been so wrapped up in work, if I had paid any attention to the crowd she was running with—" He sucked in another breath.

"Maybe she would have found some other way," Tom cut in. "Maybe she would have decided you weren't the success she wanted you to be and left you." He glanced around the small room and then zipped the duffel bag. "Maybe you would have gotten the divorce you were headed for."

For a drawn-out moment Adam struggled with his temper. He hadn't realized that Tom assessed his marriage so accurately.

"At least she'd still be alive."

Tom moved closer, clapping a hand on Adam's shoulder.

"I'm sorry," Tom said in a more subdued voice. "I just hate to see you so closed off. What happened, happened. I wish to hell you'd let go of all that blame you're carrying around and find someone special. Someone to share the kind of relationship I found with Lori." He hesitated. "How about the florist I saw you dancing with earlier? Did you already know her?"

"Yeah." Adam didn't bother to elaborate. "Isn't Lori waiting for you?" At least his sister's marriage seemed to be off to a solid start. Tom was a steady man who knew what he wanted. Sometimes Adam wished he could say the same for himself.

Tom reluctantly accepted the change of subject. "She's probably dressed by now." They shook hands again. "Thanks for everything," Tom said, opening the door as Adam handed him the duffel bag.

"I'll take care of your tux," Adam said. "Now get going, before Lori leaves without you."

"Not a chance."

As Adam followed Tom into the hallway, Lori emerged from the next room, looking fresh and pretty in her honeymoon outfit, her expression radiant. Adam was relieved to see that his new brother-in-law's attention was effectively diverted.

OVER THE NEXT couple of weeks, Diane tried not to think about Adam and the way she had felt in his arms as they danced. Her time was filled with deliveries, paperwork and, when she was lucky, odd moments to catch her breath. After closing the shop she often pursued leads or scheduled consultations with customers who wanted to establish a certain mood for a wedding or an elaborate dinner party. The hectic schedule left her only enough energy at the end of the day to return to her duplex, feed Punkin, her large orange cat, and relax with the newspaper and a hasty meal before bed. The hard work was finally beginning to pay off. Gradually Diane was building a steady clientele that seemed pleased with her skills and appreciative of her personal service.

One weak link in her operation was the temperamental station wagon she used for deliveries. She had planned to replace it when she could afford to, but an engine that made strange noises and a mechanic's estimate for a huge repair bill convinced her that the time for a replacement had come.

"There's nothing in here," Diane said disgustedly to Carol, her assistant, tossing the classified ads onto the desk. "The vans that sound promising are too expensive and the ones I can afford are probably no better than what I'm trying to replace."

"You need to do something soon," Carol said, adding a large satin bow to a wicker basket filled with peppermint-colored carnations. "We can't afford late deliveries. I'd lend you my car, but a Volkswagen Bug is hardly a solution."

"I know," Diane groaned. "If only my station wagon would hold on for a few more months."

"What about another loan?" Carol asked. She and Diane had been friends since high school, growing closer after Carol had come to work at the shop, and she knew what a tight budget Diane was on.

Diane shook her head. "No more loans."

Several days later, she was again combing the nickel ads for anything that might solve her delivery problem when Carol came waltzing into the back room looking unbearably smug.

"Hi," Diane greeted her, glancing up. "Somebody have a baby?"

Carol perched on the edge of the scarred desk. "Not exactly." When Diane refused to give in to her curiosity and question her further, Carol started humming to herself. Her fingers traced some of the deeper scratches in the desktop.

After one glance at her Cheshire cat grin, Diane folded the ads and sat back. "Okay, what's up?"

The humming stopped abruptly. "Remember I told you that my brother works at Robinson's Beverage?"

Diane nodded, puzzled. Carol's brother was younger, and she had never met him. "The place that delivers soda pop. Did he get a raise?"

"No."

Diane sighed. "Has he decided to give us free samples?"

Carol chuckled. "No. But I did ask him to keep his eyes open for a good van, and he told me that the company is selling one of theirs. It has a lot of miles on it, but he said they really take care of their vehicles."

Diane pushed her bangs back out of her eyes, making a mental note to trim them that evening. "Do they want a lot for it?"

"That's the beauty of the whole thing." Carol named a low figure.

"What's the number?" Diane asked, reaching for the phone as her assistant turned to answer the summons of the front-door chime.

A few moments later, she thanked the man at the other end and hung up. After Diane had made several more calls, Carol finally finished with her customer and came back, her face full of eager curiosity.

"So?"

Diane shook her head. "The price is reasonable enough, but there's a catch. The van has to be repainted immediately to cover their company logo. I guess that's a common practice."

"So?" Carol repeated, scooping up a small stack of orders. "What's the problem? Have one of those cheap spray jobs done."

Diane twiddled a pencil between her fingers and glanced at the figures before her. "I called around, but even a cheap paint job is more than I can afford right now. Quarterly taxes are due next week." She had called almost every place listed for prices, only confirming the fact that she couldn't afford both the van and the necessary paint job.

Early that evening, after Carol had left and Diane locked the front door behind her and turned off the showroom lights, she looked over the ledger again, trying to see if there was anything she had missed. There wasn't.

She frowned and rubbed at the dull ache in the middle of her forehead. There was one place she hadn't called, one place she had studiously avoided even thinking about. Finally she slammed the ledger shut and flipped open the phone book to the Yellow Pages.

Adam hadn't even bothered with one of the eye-catching ads like the one she paid a small fortune for each month. The only mention of his shop was a small listing in the text under Automobile Body Repair and Painting. Checking the number, Diane took a deep breath and dialed. Perhaps if she were lucky he would be gone.

The phone was answered on the fourth ring, just as she was telling herself that she had tried and could now hang up.

"Adam Westover." He sounded harried.

"This is Diane Simmons." She tried to maintain a strictly professional tone, but the memory of his devilish brown eyes got in the way, softening her voice until she spoiled the effect by clearing her throat.

Adam's tone warmed instantly. "Diane! It's good to hear from you. Change your mind about lunch?"

Oh, God. She should have known better than to call. "No," she said hastily. "I'm calling about business."

"Having a special on daisies this week?" he asked. His voice shifted again, as if he had cradled the phone into his wide shoulder. Diane could picture him leaning against the wall, his long body intriguingly masculine in snug jeans and a plaid shirt. Remembering the heady feel of his arms around her, she went tense, blinking her eyes to dissolve his image.

"No, not my business, your business."

"Oh?" He perked up with interest. "How can I help you?"

"I'm looking at a delivery van to buy," she said, wishing she had resisted the urge to call him at all. His price would probably be way over her head, and she would have endured the insistent attraction of his deep voice for nothing. He didn't speak and she forced herself to continue. "Robinson's Beverage Distributors has it for sale. The only hitch is that they want it repainted before I use it."

"Yeah," he said, "I've run into that before."

"I'm on a tight budget," she confessed reluctantly. "I need transportation but so far the bids I've gotten have been too high." Suddenly she realized that he might take her explanation as a request that he give her a special deal. Her cheeks heated.

"I'm sure your prices are high, too, and I don't want any favors." She bit her lip. "This was probably a bad idea. I'm sorry I wasted your time." Before she could change her mind, or Adam could say anything, she bid him a hasty goodbye and hung up, feeling like an utter fool. It was time to call it a night and go home to Punkin.

The phone started ringing as her hand poised over the answering machine. She stared, sure it was Adam but reluctant to miss a potential customer if it wasn't. As she stood, torn with indecision, the ringing stopped, only to start again almost immediately. It had to be him.

As soon as the phone went quiet again, Diane flipped on the machine and locked up. She was fumbling with the key to the wagon, praying it would start, when a pickup truck pulled into the small parking lot next to the shop, spraying gravel as it stopped abruptly. As the truck's lights went out, she saw Adam's name on its door. He cut the engine and emerged from the cab.

"Why didn't you answer your phone?" he asked, approaching her. "I called you right back."

"I must have had my head in the cooler," she lied, facing him squarely. "What did you want?"

Adam stopped, looking down at her with a puzzled grin. "Our conversation ended kind of suddenly. You really didn't give me much of a chance to say anything."

"I changed my mind." Diane lifted her chin defiantly.

"About getting a new delivery van?" His voice was incredulous as he looked at her wagon, the neat white sign on the driver's door a startling contrast to its faded paint.

"About getting a bid from you," she corrected him.

"That's hardly fair." Adam's voice had softened and his smile gentled. "Are you allowing personal feelings to get in the way of business?"

"What personal feelings? I don't have any personal feelings toward you." He hadn't even called her.

Adam's smile widened. "Didn't your mother ever tell you your nose would grow if you told a lie?"

The unexpected outrageousness of his comment made her smile. "Yes, but it never has," she replied. "Not that I'm lying now."

Adam continued to look down at her until Diane felt suddenly crowded. She shifted uncomfortably. Then he turned his dark head to look at the wagon again.

"Tell you what," he said, "let me go with you to look at the van you're interested in. I can give you a bid on the paint, and maybe check it out under the hood. Unless you're mechanical yourself and don't need my opinion?" He ended on a questioning note.

Diane couldn't help but laugh. "*Mechanical*, me? It's all I can do to jump start Bessie, here, when she needs it, without shorting us both out."

Adam returned his gaze to her face, and Diane forced herself to keep her voice steady, despite the increase in her pulse. She really couldn't afford to turn down his offer, not when it was for the business. But if he thought she was going to take any special favors, especially ones with strings attached, he could think again.

"I would appreciate your opinion," she said. "If I call them in the morning, could you go with me on our lunch hour?"

Adam's grin flashed dangerously and she felt her breath catch. "I thought you didn't take a lunch hour?"

"This is a special situation," she said. "Please?"

His expression sent a wave of heat from her toes right up to her cheeks. "Only if you take the time to eat with me afterward," he said.

"You drive a hard bargain." Diane thought quickly. Tomorrow was Carol's day to leave early. "Can't. I have to get back."

Adam's dark brows bunched into a frown. "You could at least *try* to look disappointed," he growled.

Diane stuck out her lower lip into an exaggerated pout. "Better?"

"Not much, but I'm a patient man."

She did her best to ignore the meaning behind his words. "Could you pick me up?" she asked instead. "I'm not sure how reliable Bessie would be, especially if she knows she might be replaced."

Adam didn't have to think twice to agree. He had managed to avoid calling Diane, but she intruded into his thoughts every day, at the most unexpected times. He had known it was only a matter of time before he broke down. Even without lunch, this was working out better than he had hoped.

He nodded and confirmed the arrangement, resisting the urge to lean down and drop a kiss onto her upturned nose. Diane's mouth was even more tempting, but thinking about tasting it was more than he could comfortably handle in the privacy of her parking lot and the gathering twilight. He knew without a shadow of a doubt that if he did give in to temptation and kiss her, he would be jeopardizing more than their "date" tomorrow.

"I'll wait while you start Bessie," he said. "Do you want me to follow you home?" He wasn't surprised when she turned down his offer. "Tomorrow, then," he said, climbing into the truck and waiting until the wagon's engine caught and Diane blinked her lights.

On his way home, Adam wondered what it was about Diane that kept poking at him. Was he interested just because she wasn't? Did he see her as a challenge? The nagging questions didn't come with any easy answers.

DIANE WOKE UP to the sound of Punkin's meows from the kitchen, then glanced at the digital alarm clock on the nightstand. Breakfast time for man and beast.

She was swinging her legs out of the warm nest of bedcovers when she remembered with a flutter of reaction that today was the day she was meeting Adam to look at the van. She ran a hand through her straight hair, mentally going over her wardrobe as she turned on the shower, then padded to the kitchen to give Punkin his breakfast.

As he began to wolf down the dried kibbles, Diane left him to it and stripped off her nightshirt. She took an extra moment to study her reflection in the mirror, wondering if she should apply more makeup than the faint pink gloss she usually put on her lips to keep them from drying out. Then she gave herself a mental shake, ran a brush through her hair and let it fall straight to her shoulders before sliding open the door to her well-organized closet and grabbing her red plaid camp shirt and denim wrap skirt.

No way was Diane altering her routine just because she was seeing Adam Westover. It was a business meeting, she reminded herself as she poured milk over cold cereal and sliced half a banana on top.

Punkin finished washing his white paws and came over to rub against Diane's legs as she ate her cereal. He purred and looked up at her adoringly with his golden eyes. He was a sweet-natured cat and got along well with everybody. Reaching down to scratch behind his ears, Diane glanced at her watch.

"Gotta run, baby. See you after work."

Punkin just stared, purring loudly as she bent to run her hand over his long soft fur. "Wish me luck," she said on her way out. She had a feeling she would need all the luck she could manage today, and she wasn't thinking only of the new van.

THE MORNING DRAGGED endlessly for Adam, even though he was working on a project he especially enjoyed, preparing a classic old Studebaker for its first coat of deep burgundy lacquer. The car's owner, a wealthy real estate broker from L.A., wanted extensive pinstriping to match the car's new white leather interior, but he had given Adam a free rein with the design.

Adam suspected that the customer, who looked to be in his fifties, was trying to recapture his youth. If the car made him feel better, Adam had no qualms about helping.

He turned off the electric sander and glanced at his watch. Only ten minutes had crawled by since the last time he had looked. With renewed determination, he lifted the sander and turned his attention to the Studebaker's rear fender.

Finally, when it seemed to him that two days must have gone by, it was time to stop and clean up for his meeting with Diane. Adam washed off the dirt in the small restroom and quickly changed into the clean jeans and shirt he had brought with him. Then he shouted to the teenage boy who did odd jobs for him, reminding him to catch the phone, and went out to his Chev, whistling tunelessly as he jangled his key chain.

Adam wondered if Diane would be impressed by the meticulously restored red and cream Bel-Air convertible, or if she would even notice it. Not for the first time, he puzzled over what made her tick, what drove her so hard and how she could maintain her schedule of work, work and more work. Or was she just pretending, using make-believe obligations to avoid him?

He shook his head as he drove the short distance to Diane's Flowers. Adam purposely kept his own schedule uncluttered, leaving plenty of time to pursue his other interests—bicycling, horseback riding, and etching on glass. More than once he had been encouraged by former customers to move his custom car painting business back to L.A., but each time he'd declined. He was making enough money in Silver Creek, and he definitely didn't want to exchange his life here for the hectic roller coaster ride of Southern California that he remembered so well.

Diane waved through the front window when she saw him pull up, said something to the woman working beside her and grabbed her purse. Adam got out and opened the passenger door as she left the shop. His gaze stayed on her until she reached his car.

"Hi," he murmured. "Nice day for a drive. Too bad you don't have more time."

"Yes," Diane agreed, returning his smile with a subdued one of her own. "But Carol, my assistant, leaves at one today."

Adam shut her door after she slid in, and circled the car. "Do you mind if I keep the top down?"

Diane glanced around, at the creamy leather upholstery and the gleaming dash of the old Chevy. Even the steering wheel looked like new.

"This is beautiful," she said, running her hand over the bench seat as he slid behind the wheel. "Did you redo it all yourself?"

"Yup. Do you really like it?"

"It reminds me of my first car, except it wasn't a convertible. And it wasn't this nice. You do beautiful work." She glanced down. Even the carpeting on the floor was spotless.

"Thanks." Her words pleased him, more than winning another trophy would.

Diane shook her straight hair and Adam noticed how it glinted in the sunlight. "I don't mind if you leave the top down, but I think this whole trip is going to be a big waste of time."

His brows rose at the sudden flatness of her tone. "What makes you so pessimistic on such a gorgeous day?" he asked, giving her a questioning look.

"If you plan for the worst, then you're pleasantly surprised if something good happens and not disappointed if it doesn't," Diane said, buckling her seat belt.

When she looked back up, Adam's expression had changed to one of astonishment. "A cynic!" he exclaimed dramatically, starting the quiet engine and pulling into the street. "And at such a tender age."

Diane glared at his profile. "If that's a subtle way of asking how old I am, I'm twenty-nine."

"I wasn't asking, but since you told me, that seems young to have your own business."

"How old are you?" she asked.

"Thirty-four, but some days I feel older."

Diane looked at his tanned arms below the short sleeves of his cotton shirt. "Somehow I doubt that you ever feel old," she said. "And you hardly look over-worked."

Adam stopped at a red light and took the opportunity to turn toward her. "I make a point not to be over-worked. Life's too short."

The light changed, and Diane snorted derisively as he accelerated. "Some of us don't have that option."

Adam was silent for a moment. "Maybe you're right. But we all make choices. You know what they say about all work and no play."

"Yeah," she said, "that's my father's creed." Her voice had a sarcastic edge to it.

"Does your family live around here?" Adam left the business district and took the main road out of town to where the beverage plant was located.

Diane nodded. "I grew up in Silver Creek. My mother still lives in the same house, and I have two younger sisters. They're both married and settled down already."

"What's wrong with that?"

"Nothing, I guess, if you lack ambition," she said.

Adam thought about that. "It must be nice to all live so close," he said finally. "You see a lot of them?"

She shrugged, remembering how long it'd been since she had taken the time to visit, or even to call. It seemed as if she was always too busy, or too tired.

"It's been a while," she admitted. "But I haven't had the time."

Adam thought of his own hardworking father, a doctor who had spent long hours establishing a successful practice in Los Angeles. He had rarely been home while Adam was growing up. After a heart attack that had been classified as a warning, he reluctantly slowed down for a short while, but now he was back to a nearly full schedule, apparently unable or unwilling to make himself do less.

Adam wouldn't trade life-styles and bank balances with his father for anything. He had traveled that same road once, but never again, after learning the hard way that success wasn't the most important thing in life. Adam refused to be chained to a job that took all of his time and energy; the cost was too high.

"There's Robinson Beverage." Diane sat up straighter. "Carol's brother, Ken, said the van would be parked at the back of the lot, and he'd meet us there at twelve-fifteen." She glanced at the plain round watch on her wrist. "It's almost that now."

After they had gotten out of Adam's car, it only took a few minutes for Diane to see that the van with the For Sale sign in the window would be perfect. While she checked out the interior, which was utilitarian but not badly worn, Adam looked over the outside, muttering to himself.

"The body's pretty straight," he said, circling the vehicle slowly. "Chips in the paint but no dents except a couple of small dings in the door."

Adam straightened as Carol's brother walked up and they all introduced themselves. Ken handed Diane the keys.

"Take it for a spin," he said, gesturing toward the open gate. "Drop the keys by the front office and let me know what you decide."

Diane glanced at Adam, who slid into the passenger seat. "Let's go."

Adam remained silent as she drove past Carol's brother and through the gates. Then she turned onto the main road, accelerating smoothly. After a little ways, she braked and turned off onto the wide shoulder. When she glanced at Adam he nodded, then she reversed, turned around and headed back the way they had come.

When she parked again, Adam got out and lifted the hood. "Put it in neutral and goose it," he shouted.

Diane obliged. When he looked up and ran a finger across his throat in a slashing motion, she shut it off. Then she got back out while he checked the tires.

"Good rubber," he mumbled, sliding the side door open and shut.

Diane was waiting anxiously. It was perfect. If only— she tried to remind herself that she wouldn't be able to afford Adam's bid. And if he set it too low she couldn't accept.

"What color?" he asked abruptly.

She looked at him with a blank expression.

"The van," he said with a grin that made her swallow hard. "What color do you want it painted?"

Diane hadn't even thought that far. "Uh, how about pink? Light pink." That seemed like a good color for a flower business.

Adam made a mock face at her, then scratched his chin and circled the van again. When he came back to her side, he studied the driver's door for a long moment.

"Pink it is," he said. "And I'll paint a garland of flowers here, with the shop's name and address in black letters inside. And of course lettering on the back, as well as the passenger side. How would that be?"

Diane's mouth almost watered. She hadn't thought about the lettering, planning instead to use the old magnetic signs from the wagon. She could picture the van filled with orders, its exterior gleaming with new paint. She took a deep breath and forced herself to ask, "How much?"

Adam thought for another long moment, then named a figure that was ridiculously low. Before Diane could sputter a protest, he held up a detaining hand.

"How about this?" he said quickly. "I'll paint in a small credit below the garland. That way I'll get some more business out of it—free advertising." His expression was totally innocent.

Diane knew he was offering her a special deal, much lower than what he must usually charge. She knew he didn't need the advertising, suspecting he probably had more work than he wanted now. She knew, too, that her pride should be strong enough to keep her from accepting a favor she could never hope to repay.

"It's a deal," she said, surprising both of them. "How soon can you have the work done?"

3

ADAM'S STUNNED expression would have been comical if Diane were in the mood to laugh. He recovered quickly, running a hand through his hair. "End of next week?"

There was no reason for her to know about the jobs he was sliding to get hers in so soon. He had a feeling that if he took any longer she would change her mind, and whether or not she ever went out with him on a real date, he decided he wanted to do this job for her. She worked so hard and needed success so badly that he wanted to help in some small way even if he didn't completely approve.

"Great," Diane said, her excitement showing for the first time. "Let's stop by the office and I'll tell them."

She chattered all the way back to her shop. All Adam had to do was to smile encouragingly each time she slowed down and she was off again, sharing her dreams of success, waving her hands as she talked. He would have guessed that with her ambition she would have wanted a string of shops; she surprised him by saying she only wanted the one she had to be solidly successful. She mentioned eventually carrying a line of dried flowers for hobbyists, or getting more green plants and pots and baskets to put them in.

When Adam stopped in the alley behind her shop, Diane abruptly went silent, looking self-conscious.

"I don't usually run on like that." Her cheeks were a betraying pink.

"I enjoyed hearing your ideas," Adam said, getting out and opening her door before she could hop out herself. "You've given this a lot of thought."

"Yes." She clipped the word off as if she were afraid to say more.

They stood awkwardly by the building's back door. Not a soul was around.

"I had better get in," Diane said. "Thank you very much." She frowned as if something weighed heavily on her mind. "I appreciate the favor," she mumbled finally, looking everywhere but at his face.

Adam started to protest, but she interrupted.

"I'm not a fool. Perhaps I should have declined, but I need the van too much. Anyway, I want you to know that as soon as I think of a way, I'll pay you back."

Adam shook his head, about to tell her it wasn't necessary. Then he realized that if he refused her offer of repayment, she might yet back out.

"You could fix me a few dinners," he suggested hopefully.

Diane narrowed her eyes and shook her head. "I don't think you'd want to eat what I could cook."

"That bad?"

She nodded. "I've never taken the time to learn. I make do with canned or frozen."

Adam shuddered at her words. He made a pretense of thinking hard. "Do you like baseball? I'd consider it a real favor if you went with me to some of the local minor league games."

Diane shook her head again. "I'm sorry," she said, not sounding the least bit sorry. "I really don't have the time."

"I'm running out of ideas," Adam said, thinking of several things he knew she would never agree to.

"*I* know," she said, snapping her fingers. "I could give you free goodbye bouquets. Every time you need one, come to me. It might take a long time to pay you back, but I'll make them really lovely...." Her voice trailed off when she glanced at his face and saw his dark frown. For a moment she was disappointed.

Then Adam managed a smile. "I don't think I'll be needing any more 'goodbye' bouquets, but thanks anyway."

Diane looked as if she expected him to explain, but he only stared pointedly and kept smiling. Color started to flood her face as his inference began to sink in.

"Well," she said briskly, "that's up to you. I don't know what else to offer."

Adam threw up his arms in mock exasperation, glancing quickly around. The alley was still deserted.

"Okay," he said with a sigh. "If you insist on paying me back, and none of my other suggestions suit you, I guess we'll just have to resort to this."

Before Diane could utter a protest, he pulled her into his arms. The last thing she saw before her eyes fluttered shut was the sudden gleam in his.

Adam's mouth settled on hers, warm and coaxing. Caught totally off guard, Diane responded to the kiss. Her hands, with a will of their own, curled around his neck. Adam pulled her even closer, and she melted against his tall body. The world behind her closed lids was spinning with colored lights, and everything had receded but him.

He finally lifted his mouth from hers and she murmured a protest. Before she could come to her senses and jerk out of his embrace, he dropped his arms and stepped away. Diane's eyes flew open, and her fingers went to her tingling lips.

Adam's eyes were almost black, but his expression could only be described as triumphant. "Consider your debt paid in full," he murmured softly.

Before Diane had a chance to react, Adam quickly moved to his car and slid behind the wheel. As she watched, speechless, he started the motor, shifted into reverse and slowly drove away. Diane turned around and stomped back into the shop. She resented everything about him, his arrogance, his attitude toward success, even the dimple that appeared when he flashed her a devilish grin. And the worst thing was that she was attracted to him. Very attracted.

Diane believed that success would come with hard work; Adam didn't appreciate financial success, or ambition. Instead he practically gave away his services, at least to her. That reminded her of his idea of repayment. Her lips tingled and her cheeks burned. What was it about Adam Westover that infuriated her so?

"Back already?" Carol asked, glancing toward the doorway where Diane had stopped to banish Adam from her thoughts. "I thought you might be later, with someone like that to keep you company."

There was a question in Carol's voice that Diane ignored as she walked over to the counter. Her assistant was always telling her she worked too hard. Saying anything to Carol about Adam would only give her additional fuel.

"I figured you'd want to get out of here on time."

"What about the van?" Carol asked. "Any luck?"

Diane paused dramatically, then couldn't hold back a grin. "Yes! It's perfect."

Carol clapped her hands. "Wonderful! When do we get it? What color are you having it painted? Are you going to sell the wagon?"

Carol's enthusiasm was contagious. Diane's voice betrayed her own excitement as she answered, "I'm not sure when we'll get it—the color is pink—and I don't know if I'll sell the wagon." She took a steadying breath. "Anything else for now?"

Carol shook her head and grabbed her purse from behind the counter. "Your messages are on the pad," she said. "It's been pretty slow."

Diane's good mood evaporated. That wasn't what she wanted to hear. "See you tomorrow, then."

Carol must have picked up on the flatness of her voice. "This afternoon will be busier," she said as she pushed open the door. "Congrats on the van."

Diane wished her goodbye and picked up the message pad.

SHE DIDN'T SEE or hear from Adam until the middle of the next week. Her work had picked up as it always did toward the weekend, and she told herself she was glad he didn't come around to bother her. Still, he could have picked up the phone and told her how the paint job was going.

Diane had just taken an order for a dozen red roses to be delivered to the local hospital the next morning when she heard a car pull into the gravel parking lot. Writing down the rest of the order, she glanced through the window.

And froze.

There outside was her van, and it was breathtaking. Diane walked toward the door, hardly aware she was moving. Adam climbed out of the van and waved. She barely spared him a glance as she went outside and circled it slowly.

It looked brand-new—the body perfect and the pale pink paint exactly the way she had pictured it, an elegant background to the garland of roses and daisies circling the bold black script on the driver's door that Adam had shut behind him.

The business name and address were repeated on the passenger side and the back, across the van's double doors. There Adam had painted a few scattered flowers, as if they'd been dropped as the van pulled away.

Swallowing, Diane did her best to subdue the excitement that bubbled within her. It might only encourage Adam in his romantic pursuit if he knew how thrilled she was.

"It's very nice," she said, coming back around to where he was standing, one hand shoved into the back pocket of his paint-stained jeans. "Thanks for getting it done so quickly."

Diane almost felt regret when the eager light faded from his dark eyes. "I'm glad you like it," he said in an equally steady voice.

Adam did his best not to let his disappointment show as visions of Diane gratefully throwing herself into his arms dissolved in the harsh light of reality. Perhaps she just wasn't a demonstrative person.

Perhaps he had been mistaken, and she really didn't return his interest.

He stood back and watched silently as she bent closer to examine the brushwork on the driver's door. Adam was proud of the circlet of daisies and roses—two items he didn't get much call to paint on the cars he customized.

"I like the way you did the lettering," Diane said. "This script is classy but easy to read. Did you stencil it?"

Adam stiffened, doing his best not to appear offended by her accidental slur. *Stencil?*

"No, I always do the lettering freehand. I've had a lot of practice."

She glanced up at him, violet eyes working their spell. "I suppose you have." Her hand skimmed down the door, feeling the utter smoothness of the finish.

Adam thought about that delicate hand running over his skin, and shifted uncomfortably. "I adjusted the door catches," he pointed out, trying to distract himself, "and cleaned out the interior."

Diane's expression was one of surprise as she opened and shut one of the back doors. "You didn't have to do that."

Adam shrugged. "I had the time."

Diane wondered how many jobs he'd turned down while he had been working on her van. For pauper's wages. She made herself go over and touch his arm. "I really appreciate what you've done," she said quietly. "It's a beautiful job."

Adam's skin was warm and alive beneath her fingers. His dark eyes narrowed as she withdrew, and his gaze flicked to her mouth. She backed away hastily, resisting the urge to blow on her fingers to cool them. "Do you want the money now?"

He blinked. "No. My bookkeeper will send you a statement." He handed her the keys to the van.

Her hand closed around them. They were warm from his touch. "Oh. Okay."

The silence between them stretched taut. Adam seemed to be waiting for something else. Nervously,

Diane glanced again at the van. "It looks great," she repeated.

For some reason, her words seemed to irritate him. "Good," he said shortly, turning away.

"Can I give you a ride back to your shop?" Diane asked, not sure what had just happened to make him frown.

He shook his head. "I need the exercise."

She watched him walk away. "Thanks again," she called when he didn't look back.

He waved without turning, his boots crunching on the gravel.

Diane almost forgot about him as she opened the van's door and climbed into the driver's seat, looking out the windshield and picturing herself delivering orders while pedestrians and other drivers watched with envy. She was turning the steering wheel and making soft engine noises when a voice beside the open window made her jump.

"This is gorgeous, a lot nicer than I'd pictured," Carol said.

Embarrassed at being caught playacting, Diane got down. She waited while Carol admired the van from every angle. "This will give the business some extra class," she said.

"It turned out pretty nice, didn't it?"

Before Carol could reply, the phone inside the shop began to ring. "I'll get it." She dashed back inside.

Diane followed more slowly, puzzling over Adam's abrupt change of mood. She'd thanked him and admired his work. What else did he expect? Shrugging, she went inside, instinct telling her he'd been waiting for something specific.

Back at his own business, Adam began looking through his scheduled orders, trying to ignore his feeling of dejection. What had he expected, anyway? Diane thanked him, had seemed to like the way the van turned out. What else did he want? And why did he even care?

He remembered the kiss. That had been a bad mistake, a tactical error. He had meant to give her something to think about and instead *he* was the one who couldn't get *her* out of his mind. Despite the inner voice that was urging caution, he was more determined than ever to get a reaction from cool, hardworking Diane Simmons. He wanted to be the one to break her concentration, to distract her from her all-consuming desire to work herself into the ground. He wanted to see some of the hunger he had felt ever since he'd held her in his arms at the wedding, reflected in her deep blue eyes. Damn it, he wanted her.

Maybe directness wasn't his best plan. Maybe Diane would react better to subtlety, to romance. An idea occurred to him, and he thought about it as he absently glanced through the mail. A smile quirked the corners of Adam's mouth as he studied the brochure for a new line of paints. Yeah, he thought, rubbing his chin. That just might work.

"I HAVEN'T SEEN Mister Red Convertible around," Carol said as she snipped the ends from some long-stemmed pink carnations and arranged them in a tall green vase.

Diane, who was sitting at the counter sorting invoices, shrugged. "Me, neither. I guess he's busy."

Carol sighed. "You need more in your life than your business and your cat."

"I don't have time for anything else," Diane said stubbornly. "I barely have time for my family, and I certainly don't have time for some fender-straightener who doesn't even take his business seriously."

"How do you know that?" Carol asked, coaxing candy-striped ribbon into an elaborate bow. "He sure did a great job on the van."

Diane gave up on the invoices. "I didn't mean that he doesn't do good work. I just meant he doesn't seem to have any ambition." She clipped the pile of papers together and set them aside. "Half the time his shop is closed."

Carol gave her a piercing look. "I didn't know you had any reason to go down his street."

Diane blushed. "I just got bored, always going home the same way."

Carol was kind enough not to comment on her lame excuse. "Well, he seems nice enough," she said, attaching the card and a copy of the order to the bouquet she had just finished and setting it in the cooler. "Sometimes a man being single is enough to get him consideration in this town." Carol had a longtime boyfriend who traveled a lot in his work.

"If a woman's looking," Diane commented shortly.

"Right," Carol drawled as she went into the storeroom. "I'm going to check on the vases, see if we need to reorder," she called as the door swung shut behind her.

Diane picked up the stack of invoices, deciding to finish them after all, when the front door opened, the little bell above it tinkling merrily. She tried not to react to the sight of Adam striding toward her, but her body ignored her instructions, as her nerves snapped to attention, and heat suffused her cheeks. It had been days since she'd seen him and she had begun to think he'd finally given up.

"Hi," she greeted him, attempting coolness.

"Hi. How's the van working out?" He looked as tempting as ever, standing there in his usual snug jeans with a plaid cotton shirt that made his broad shoulders look wider and his tanned forearms darker. It was obvious from the rich shade of his skin that he spent a lot of time outdoors. Diane felt pale and unattractive in comparison.

Adam shifted his weight to one hip. Diane's gaze hovered in the vicinity below his belt buckle, then she dragged her attention to his question. "The van's fine. It runs well and it doesn't take near the gas my wagon did."

Adam nodded. "Glad to hear it."

"So what can I do for you?" she asked, preparing herself to withstand another assault on her senses.

"I need to order some flowers, something really nice," he said, surprising her.

With a great effort of will, Diane kept the smile plastered on her face. "What did you have in mind?" Perhaps it was his mother's birthday.

He thought a moment. "I want something romantic."

Her theory about his mother faded.

"Flowers with a nice scent, I guess. Maybe some carnations. They smell pretty. But something big, a bouquet that will really impress the woman I'm sending it to." He demonstrated in the air with his hands. "You know what I mean?"

Diane's heart sank. He'd met someone. That was why he hadn't been around. She should count herself lucky that he'd painted her van before he lost interest. Squaring her shoulders, she led him to the cooler.

"Roses are always nice, or a mixed bouquet." She pointed to a bucket of tall gladioli. "These are really fresh."

"They remind me of funerals," he said, studying them. "And weddings." He scratched his chin. "I want something really—" for a moment he looked perplexed "—old-fashioned. Feminine," he said. "A bouquet that looks like I gathered it myself."

Understanding what he meant, Diane quickly suggested a mixture of flowers and colors, doing her best to squash any personal feelings. When she glanced at him, Adam agreed to everything she suggested.

"Put them in that crystal vase," he said, pointing, "and put a big bow around it. Pink. The lady likes pink."

It was all Diane could do not to grind her teeth. How unfeeling of him to ask *her* to do this. "The vase is extra," she pointed out. "It's imported lead crystal."

"No problem." He looked extremely pleased with himself.

Diane tried not to frown. She was not a violent person, so why did the impulse to slap the smile from his face carry so much appeal? "Do you want to pick it up or shall I deliver it?"

If anything, his grin widened. "Maybe I should have it delivered," he mused.

Damn him, he was enjoying this. Fury boiled inside her.

She laid a small envelope on the counter. "Fill out a card and write her address on this." Only a little of what she was feeling seeped into her voice.

For a moment Adam studied her. *Just get this over with and go,* she urged silently, glaring back. His dimple flashed and his teeth were white against his tan skin. He looked absolutely devastating. It shouldn't surprise her that he had found someone else so quickly.

The lucky woman would be bowled over by the flowers. Diane's handiwork! She wondered how this new quarry would feel when she got another bunch, a goodbye bouquet when Adam was tired of her. *Diane* hadn't even gotten that. Their relationship, if it could loosely be called one, hadn't progressed that far.

She watched him stealthily as he picked out a card with a cupid and hearts across the top. *Just because,* it said in elaborate script. *You know why,* Adam wrote in his bold handwriting. *Love, A.*

Diane couldn't wrench her gaze away as he picked up the envelope. A mixture of emotions sizzled through her. Well, she'd had her chance. A chance she hadn't even realized she'd wanted.

Adam was holding the pen, absently looking down at the blank envelope. Impatiently, Diane began to drum her fingers on the counter.

"Can't remember her name?"

He chuckled. "No, I don't know the address." His dark gaze bored into hers. "Why don't you write it for me?" He slid the envelope toward her.

"How would *I* know it?" she demanded, barely suppressing her annoyance.

"Don't you know where you live?"

Diane stared, blinking uncomprehendingly.

Adam's hand curled around hers as he put the pen into her fingers. "I thought you would have guessed," he said quietly, all traces of amusement wiped from his face. "The flowers are for you."

Diane continued to stare. He seemed to be waiting again.

"For me?" she echoed.

He nodded and his attractive mouth curved upward at the corners. "That's right."

"A goodbye bouquet?" she asked.

His gaze dropped to her mouth, singeing the tender flesh. "Lady, this is as far from a goodbye bouquet as you'll ever get."

Diane swallowed. "I don't know what to say." She was glad that Carol was still in the back room.

"Say 'thank you, Adam.'"

"Thank you, Adam," she parroted, coloring with embarrassment.

He came around the counter, crowding her. "Shall I deliver them personally or would you rather take them home with you?"

There was no way that Diane could resist being flattered by his persistence. "What would you rather do?" she almost whispered.

Adam's hand came up to skim over her cheek and along her jaw in a caress she felt to her toes. "Would you have dinner with me tonight?"

Speechless, she bobbed her head then swayed toward the warmth of his touch on her skin, hypnotized by the glitter of his dark eyes. His other hand was reaching out when Carol burst through the door to the back room, waving a piece of paper.

"I've got the vases inventoried," she said, then stopped abruptly, looking flustered.

Regaining her equilibrium, Diane performed hasty introductions.

After telling Adam what a wonderful job she thought he'd done on the van and casting an approving glance at Diane, Carol fluttered the paper she'd been holding. "I was going to call the vase order in while I'm thinking about it." Her expression was questioning.

"How about giving me a quick tour?" Adam suggested to Diane, still affected by the way she'd been looking at him. If he didn't get to hold her again soon, he was going to explode.

"Sure." She gestured to Carol. "Go ahead and call."

Diane pointed out some things in the main area, the cooler that he had already seen, green plants swathed in jewel-toned foil or ceramic planters, rolls of ribbon in every imaginable color. Then she led him to the back room. One wall was covered with crowded shelves. There were boxes and vases and pots stacked all over, and equipment everywhere, including several odd-shaped lattice work structures painted white.

"We use those in weddings, mostly," Diane said. She pointed to a closed door. "Restroom's in there."

Then she turned to Adam, who was standing close behind her. "That's about it."

"Very nice," he murmured, wondering if Carol would have the good sense to stay out front.

The air between them became charged with tension.

"About dinner," he began.

"Sounds great." Her easy capitulation surprised him. He had expected an argument.

"I'll pick you up at seven. We'll go somewhere casual, okay?"

Diane nodded. She was so close that her perfume, something light and floral, teased his nostrils. Her golden hair fell straight to her shoulders, shimmering, and her bangs brushed against the darker wings of her brows as she looked directly into his eyes.

As if with a mind of its own, his hand lifted to her slightly pointed chin, his finger crooking to tip it upward. He bent his head, senses swimming with her scents and colors.

Adam half expected her to pull away, but she didn't. Moving slowly, he touched his mouth to hers. He felt her sigh as his arms slid around her, and he pressed her lips more firmly. She returned the kiss, moving her mouth against his. She was almost unbearably soft and warm. What Adam had meant as a simple kiss heated quickly.

Then overheated.

He traced her lips with the tip of his tongue, eager to know her taste. When she opened to him he changed the angle of the kiss, taking it deeper. Together they were sucked into a whirlpool of desire.

Diane's hands had been flat against his chest. Now her fingers curled into the fabric of his shirt, as if anchoring him closer. His arms tightened around her slim body and he was painfully aware of her hips and thighs pressing against his.

He lifted his mouth, raking in a ragged breath. As he was about to kiss her again, the ring of the phone from out front brought them both abruptly to earth.

Dropping her hands, Diane pulled back. Adam reluctantly let her go. He stared into her eyes, a deep, pure violet, without spots or shafts of another color.

"Thanks for the tour," he said, voice rough. "You've got a nice place here."

Diane didn't answer. Her expression was wary, her lips reddened.

"I'll see you at seven," he felt compelled to remind her, half afraid she'd back out.

"Okay." She started to turn away and then hesitated. "I'd better give you my address," she said, smiling faintly. Bending to the cluttered desk, she scribbled on a piece of paper. "It's easy to find."

His fingers closed over it. "I know where this is."

When they went through the doorway, Carol looked relieved and held out the telephone receiver to Diane. "Phone for you. Sorry."

"That's okay," Diane said hastily. "Adam's just going." She took the receiver and looked at him expectantly.

Adam picked a daisy up from the worktable and leaned forward to thread it above her ear. "See you later."

For a moment their gazes caught and clung. "Thanks for the flowers." Diane returned his smile.

"I'll be back for them before you close and I'll deliver them myself," he promised, glancing at Carol, who looked utterly confused. "Diane can explain. Nice meeting you."

He went out to his truck, whistling softly, wondering how badly the time was going to drag until seven.

"YOU'LL LIKE HIM," Diane told Punkin, who was rubbing against her leg as she dished up his supper. She had no worries about the cat; he liked everyone. Remembering the way Adam had kissed her and how she had responded, she was more nervous about actually going out with him for the first time than about what her cat thought.

Adam. The man she didn't want to get involved with.

Absently she set Punkin's dish on the floor. He stopped meowing and began to eagerly gulp down the Seafood Delight.

Diane sighed and glanced at the clock. Enough time for a shower before she put on something suited to a casual dinner.

Moments later she was smoothing rose-scented lotion into her damp skin while her curling iron heated. She didn't usually take the time for such niceties, but tonight was an exception.

"You have a business to run," she lectured herself in front of the steamed-up bathroom mirror. "No time for Lotharios who give out distracting kisses."

She licked her finger and touched it to the wand of her curling iron. The light sizzle told her it was ready. Quickly she set about flipping up the ends of her straight hair.

Hoping that Adam's idea of casual was the same as her own, she slipped into a softly gathered red print skirt and a white eyelet peasant blouse. She put gold hoops in her ears and red canvas sandals on her feet. A quick spritz of scent, a little mascara to darken her lashes, some softly tinted lip gloss and she was ready.

Ten minutes later the doorbell rang. Punkin raced to the door, waiting impatiently for Diane to open it.

"It's okay," she told him. "It's Adam."

Punkin leapt onto a living-room chair as she opened the door.

"Hi." Suddenly Diane felt shy.

Adam, who she was relieved to see was wearing a neatly pressed sportshirt and light slacks, let his gaze wander over her before echoing her greeting. He handed her the arrangement he'd picked up earlier in its crystal vase trimmed with pink ribbon.

Diane drew in the flowers' fragrant scent and thanked him, stepping back. "Come in." She shut the door behind Adam before setting the flowers down on the coffee table. "That's my cat, Punkin. My father gave him to me when he was a kitten."

Adam moved toward Punkin with his hand extended, palm up. "Nice kitty."

Punkin responded by spitting at him, ears flattened and tail flared out like a stick of orange cotton candy. Surprised, Adam pulled back.

Punkin jumped down from the chair and hurried toward the bedroom, a growl rumbling in his throat.

"He's never done that before," Diane exclaimed. "He likes everyone."

"He doesn't like me." Adam was frowning.

Diane looked at him, wondering if he had some terrible character flaw she had somehow overlooked.

"Don't worry," Adam said. "I'll win him over. Animals like me, and I like them."

Diane shrugged. "Okay. I'm sorry he was rude."

"No matter," Adam said. "You look lovely. I hope you're hungry. I'm starved. Do you like Mexican?"

Diane picked up her purse. "Love it. Where are we going?"

Adam told her while she pulled the door shut behind them and walked down the steps with him, her hand tucked into his. Glancing up, Diane saw a gleaming black Porsche waiting at the curb.

"Is that yours?"

"Yep. I bought it from a junkyard and restored it. The passenger side was really crunched. I thought you might like a ride before I sell it."

She stopped and he opened her door. "It's beautiful." There wasn't a hint of damage to the car's gleaming body. "Thanks," she said as she settled herself into the bucket seat while Adam circled the car and joined her. The dash was some dark wood, polished to a high gleam. "Aren't you tempted to keep it?" she asked as they pulled away from the curb.

"No, I had a Porsche when I lived in L.A. There are cars I like better."

"I didn't know you were from L.A.," Diane said, running a hand over the black leather upholstery. "How long have you lived here?"

He shrugged, watching the road. "A couple years."

"Why'd you pick Silver Creek?"

"I had visited a college buddy here and liked the town. You remember Tom Braddock, the guy who married my sister?"

How could Diane forget *that* wedding? "Oh, yes. But how did you know she'd be living here?"

"I didn't. I decided to move here after my marriage ended, and Lori was visiting me when she met Tom. The rest, as they say, is history." He glanced at her and smiled. "Instant lust," he said in a teasing voice.

"You mean love, don't you?"

He chuckled. "Probably."

"Don't you believe in love?" Diane teased back as he pulled into a parking lot and shut off the engine. She wondered about the marriage he'd mentioned so briefly but she didn't quite have the nerve to question him.

Adam turned to her, a crooked smile on his mouth. "I believe in love more all the time."

IT WAS STILL EARLY when he drove Diane back to her apartment. He had enjoyed the dinner and their conversation. They had some similar interests and, although they disagreed on more than one subject, he found he even liked arguing with her.

Beside him, Diane hummed softly to the radio. Apparently the silence between them didn't bother her. Most of the women he knew would have been trying to fill it with chatter.

What bothered Adam was that remark about love that had come out of his mouth earlier without a thought behind it. Diane, slightly flustered, had merely looked away, asking if he had restored the dash and interior of the Porsche, too.

For the life of him, Adam wasn't sure what he had meant to imply with the comment. He knew how painful emotional commitment could be, and he had managed to avoid it since his wife's sudden death. He hadn't changed his opinion, but his interest in Diane grew stronger each time they were together. Sooner or later he would have to put a stop to it, for his own self-preservation.

Just not yet, a voice inside Adam whispered as they pulled up in front of her apartment. *Not yet*.

4

"Want to come in for a minute?" Diane asked as Adam politely opened her car door. "I could make some coffee."

Her expectant smile faded when he shook his head. "I've got paperwork to finish," he told her, feeling guilty. He did have paperwork, but he had the rest of the week to get it ready for the bookkeeper.

"I'll walk you up." He cupped her elbow, refusing to think about her apparent disappointment, or his own.

Still, despite his best resolutions, he followed her inside when she had unlocked her front door, and slid his hands around her waist.

Diane stepped closer, tilting back her head. Adam covered her mouth with his, and her response sent him reeling. Heat poured through him as her lips parted and her tongue met his in a sensual dance.

Diane slid her hands up his shirt front and around his neck as he urged her closer. The feel of her soft breasts against his chest weakened his control. He groaned, his lips nibbling down her jaw to find the satiny skin behind her ear, then moving on to bury themselves in the warmth at the base of her throat.

The wide neckline of Diane's peasant blouse invited him to explore further, and his fingers closed over one breast as she stiffened and then pressed against his hand. Through the material his thumb brushed over the hardened tip, his body shuddering as it reacted instantly to the feel of her.

His control slipped even more as he returned to her mouth, kissing her harder and more intensely. Through the daze of passion a new sound intruded. He almost managed to ignore it, but Diane was already pulling away. Dimly, as Adam released her reluctantly, he was aware that the sound was a growl.

Blinking, he suppressed a sigh. The damned cat was at eye level, peering at Adam from his perch on the bookshelf, his gold eyes wide. At that moment Adam would have liked nothing better than to wring the animal's neck. As he stared, Punkin blinked slowly and began to wash one paw.

Diane shifted in his arms. "Sure you don't want that coffee?" she asked in a shaky voice.

Adam swallowed as he gazed at her flushed cheeks. One more kiss and he couldn't guarantee he wouldn't try to take things further. Neither of them was ready for that.

"No, thanks. I'd better go."

Diane's gaze mirrored his own reluctance. "Okay."

"I'll see you." Adam darted another glance at the bookcase. Punkin was nowhere in sight.

"Thanks for dinner," Diane said, following him to the door. "And the flowers."

"Perhaps giving flowers to a florist is redundant." He paused in the doorway.

She shook her head. If she had any thoughts on the way he had tricked her, she kept them to herself. "Not for this florist. I love flowers or I wouldn't be in the business."

"Good." Leaning forward to kiss her cheek, Adam drew in a last breath of her scent and went down the

steps. Before he got into the Porsche, he glanced up to
wave. The door was shut, but he thought he saw Diane
standing back from the window, watching him.

THE NEXT WEEKEND, Adam and his brother-in-law,
Tom, went for a long bicycle ride along back roads
outside Silver Creek. The two men had ridden back to
Adam's pickup and were loading the bikes when Tom
reopened a subject he'd tried to bring up earlier without much success.

"Will you tell me about the woman you've got the hot
date with tonight if I swear I won't breathe a word to
Lori?" he asked as Adam closed the tailgate and began
a series of stretching exercises. "And don't tell me you
don't have big plans this evening. No one looks at his
watch as often as you have today just because he has a
date with his television and a bowl of popcorn."

Adam leaned forward with one leg extended behind
him. He hadn't realized he'd been so obvious, and he
had forgotten how persistent Tom could be. Turning his
head to look at his friend, Adam grunted, "Good thing
you aren't a private eye. You're not even warm."

"Pull the other one." Tom sat on the grass with his
feet out in front of him. "I can smell it on you."

"That's sweat you smell."

Tom leaned forward to touch his head to one knee.
"I'm glad you're finally showing an interest in someone," he mumbled. "You can't live like a monk forever."

Adam straightened, keeping a tight control on his
emotions. Tom was only trying to help. But Adam had
hardly been living like a monk; he had just been careful not to get involved with anyone. It kept things sim-
pler that way.

"Just because you've never tried the monk's life, don't knock it," he told Tom kiddingly.

Tom got to his feet, mopping at his face with the towel that hung around his neck. "You know what I mean," he said sternly. "One-night stands and casual affairs aren't exactly involvement. They're like popcorn. A little's okay but too much will give you one hell of a gut ache."

"Talk about pop philosophy," Adam said. "Did you read that in a Batman comic book?"

Tom gestured with his hand. "Don't think I'm giving up on you, just because you managed to dodge my questions this time."

Suddenly Adam tired of the game. "Look," he said, "you can save your breath. I know you think you're helping me, but I'm fine the way I am. I learned a hard lesson, but I learned it well. While I was being the driven workaholic, my wife took an overdose of drugs that killed her. I could have stopped it, but I was too busy." He sucked in another breath.

"It's not your fault," Tom cut in. "You have to let her go and get on with your life." He raked an impatient hand through his hair. "Scary as the idea is."

For a drawn-out moment there was silence, broken only by the cry of a distant bird, as Adam absorbed Tom's words. Turning away, he fished for the truck keys in the pocket of his cutoff jeans. "I'm not scared of commitment, I'm just not interested."

Tom moved closer.

"Okay, man. Sorry if I stepped on your toes."

"Yeah, I know." Adam checked the bikes to see that they were secure and walked around to the cab. At least his sister's marriage seemed to be off to a solid start. He unlocked the driver's door of his pickup, thinking of

Diane and his date with her that evening. Unable to suppress a sudden grin, he said, "I'm dating someone."

Tom started to say something and Adam shook his head warningly. "I don't want to talk about it yet, okay?" He slid behind the wheel.

After Tom got in, he shrugged and returned Adam's grin. "Sure."

Later, when Adam had dropped Tom off and pulled up before his own small apartment, he took the front steps two at a time, looking forward to his date with Diane even as he told himself there couldn't be anything really serious between them. They were going to the car races in the next town and he had just enough time to shower and change. Pushing open the front door, he noticed that the message light on his recorder was flashing. He played the tape while downing a can of cold soda from his fridge.

Diane's voice came over the machine. "I'm sorry to cancel," she said.

His good mood evaporated.

"Something's come up at work, and I can't get away this evening. I'm really sorry."

Adam sank into a chair, swearing as he crumpled the empty pop can. He knew that Diane worked most Saturdays and he hoped that nothing serious had happened, but on the other hand, he was damned disappointed. His first impulse was to call her, or go by the shop and see what had happened. Then he decided to give her some space. If she was that busy, she didn't need interruptions.

With a disgruntled sigh, Adam thought about going to the races anyway. Chances were he'd see people he knew, and he usually enjoyed watching the stock car drivers using their speed and skill against each other.

Some of the cars carried his handiwork in their colorful paint jobs, and a visit to the pits usually got him more business.

Deciding he wasn't in the mood for the track after all, he reached for the *TV Guide*, remembering Tom's words about television and popcorn. He would much rather be spending the evening with Diane. Maybe if he stayed home, she would call later.

While he was scanning the listings, Diane was bent over the books at the shop, trying to make sense out of the sales journal. She could have left it until the next day but she knew from experience that she would have been going over and over that one page in her mind, wondering why it wouldn't balance. No, it was better to get it done this evening, along with the stack of accounts she needed to bill.

There would be enough to do the next day without paperwork. Laundry, cleaning and grocery shopping were always waiting for whenever she had a free moment. If she put off her housekeeping chores much longer, Punkin would be playing with the dust balls under the kitchen table.

The disappointment she felt over not seeing Adam that evening was determinedly thrust aside. She didn't have time for involvement; this relationship would have to stay in the compartment she had allotted it or there would be trouble.

Diane's own father had been content to work at the same blue-collar job for over thirty years, trading ambition for the security of a regular paycheck that never seemed to stretch far enough to include more than the basic necessities. She knew that financial success came with guts, hard work and sacrifice, as well as being willing to take chances, and she was determined to have a successful business no matter what the cost to her personal life. Adam would be a pleasant diversion but not a distraction. If he got in the way of her plans, he would have to go.

Diane ignored the spasm of pain she felt at the idea of not seeing him anymore. Already he had become too important to her. Maybe tonight's cancellation was a way of testing herself to see what really came first. She breathed a sigh of relief. It was Diane's Flowers that mattered to her, proving she was first and foremost a businesswoman.

She glanced at the clock, thinking about calling Adam again and quickly discarding the idea. If the truth be told, she had been relieved to leave a message on his machine. Much easier than facing him, though she would probably have to eventually. She just hoped he wouldn't show up at the shop this evening.

With renewed determination, she turned her attention back to the sales journal, poising her fingers over the calculator keys. Someday when she was secure and successful, Diane would have a computer and a bookkeeper to do the paperwork, leaving her free to concentrate on creating the floral masterpieces she so enjoyed doing.

ADAM SLAMMED DOWN his office telephone angrily. Not only had the last weekend been lonely after Diane canceled their date but he hadn't seen her since. She'd been out of the shop making deliveries both times he had stopped by, and to top it all off, she had just called to cancel the plans he'd managed to make with her for the coming weekend. Same old excuse—something had come up at work. He couldn't believe she was that busy.

Perhaps she was trying to tell him something, that the interest between them was all on his side.

He paced the floor of his small cluttered office, hands knotted into fists to keep from throwing something at the bare plasterboard wall. No, damn it, he *knew* she wasn't indifferent to him. The way she had returned his kisses proved it.

Maybe she was too interested. He dropped into the chair and propped his feet up on the scarred desk, staring blindly at a framed photograph of one of the first cars he'd repainted, a candy-apple red '57 Thunderbird with matching upholstery and wire wheels.

Was he being overconfident about his own appeal? When it came to Diane, he didn't think so. Maybe she was cautious, even reluctant to get involved, just as he was. Lord knew he was breaking the rules he'd set down for himself after Penny had died and he'd left L.A.

He knew that involvement could bring pain, that overwork could twist his values and that emotional dependence could be dangerous, even fatal. Sometimes he wondered if his attraction to Diane was the age-old male response to a challenge. The more she resisted him, the more determined he had become.

His feet dropped to the floor and he came forward in the chair with a crash, banging his fist on the desk. No! It was more than some macho knee-jerk reaction. He knew with burning certainty that it was Diane herself who interested him, not merely the challenge of winning her.

Even though winning her could be very sweet, he mused, remembering the way she'd crowded closer, returning his kiss. Very sweet, indeed. He shifted in the chair, suddenly uncomfortable with the fit of his jeans.

Adam's feelings toward her weren't all physical, either. She was bright and ambitious. Below that organized exterior lurked a hint of vulnerability that intrigued him as much as it concerned him. She was so determined to succeed, so driven that he couldn't help but fear for her. What would happen if she failed? Better not to knock yourself out, better to do what you had to without lofty dreams of dizzying success. He wished there was some way he could convince her that single-minded success wasn't always worth the price.

He doubted that at this point she would listen to the advice of someone who had been there. *He* wouldn't have, until it hit him in the face. Hard. He rose from the creaking chair. He hadn't been able to help his wife when she needed him the most; what made him think he could be any good to Diane?

AFTER ADAM had spent another lonely weekend partly alleviated by a friendly dinner with Lori and Tom, he decided it was time for action.

He had called Diane several times. Either he'd been told by Carol that she wasn't there or, if he was lucky enough to talk to Diane herself, she'd turned down his invitations with painful predictability. Today he would have it out with her. Never mind calling, he'd see her face-to-face and ask where they stood. And he would abide by her answer, no matter what it was.

He thought about going by her shop and then decided against it. Despite the fact he'd been wearing coveralls to work on a current job of his own, he had managed to get filthy and he badly needed a shower. First he would go home and clean up, have something to eat and give her the chance to do the same. Then he would go to her apartment and confront her.

The only thing was, she wasn't home when he finally got there. After he'd rung the doorbell he noticed a neighbor peering at him from behind closed curtains. Adam was tempted to wave, but didn't. Instead he jammed his hands into his pockets and turned away.

Maybe she was out with someone else.

The thought was enough to make him hesitate on the way back to his Chevy. For a moment he felt absolutely murderous. Then he realized that Diane was probably still at her shop, making do with a dry bologna sandwich while she tried to get caught up on paperwork. Adam recalled with painful clarity the similar evenings he had spent in L.A. After a moment, he snapped his fingers and hurried to his car.

DIANE LEANED BACK in the ancient steno chair and tossed down her pencil, eyeing the sandwich she'd packed that morning with a total lack of interest. Even though she only had another half hour's work ahead of her, she needed a break. The numbers were beginning to dance before her tired eyes.

Standing up, she absently rubbed the curve of her spine where it was beginning to ache. As she did, a knock sounded on the back door, startling her. She had always felt perfectly safe at the shop in the evening, even though the neighborhood of small businesses was usually deserted by six. After all, she could always phone for help if she needed it.

Still, she moved cautiously to the door and, instead of yanking it open, called out.

"Who's there?"

"It's me, Adam."

"Adam?" she echoed with mixed surprise and pleasure. She had wondered if he would just give up after all the times she'd had to refuse his company lately. Only now did she admit to herself the full extent to which she had missed him. Not taking the time to analyze her feelings, she unlocked the door and threw it open, a greeting on her lips. Then she stopped. In one hand Adam was balancing what was obviously a large pizza box. In the other he held two bottles of beer, dripping condensation.

Diane swallowed, mouth watering at the aromas wafting her way through the cardboard. Then her eyes met Adam's. He was smiling.

"May I come in?" he asked when she didn't speak.

"Of course!" She stepped aside, clearing the papers from her desk. "Set it down here."

"There are napkins in the box," he said, gaze raking over her. "I thought you might need a hot meal." It was all he could do not to drop the pizza and pull her into his arms. Only his inbred caution enabled him to resist the desire. He hadn't known if she would welcome him or not and, despite his telling himself otherwise, he did wonder if she had been trying to get rid of him.

When he set down the pizza and beer, Diane answered his unspoken question by throwing her arms around his neck.

"How did you know?" she demanded, laughing as she peered up at him.

Not one to miss an opportunity, Adam wrapped his own arms around her waist, pulling her closer. "Know what?" he mumbled, burying his face in her hair. She had missed him, too!

"That I had just decided I couldn't face another cold ham and cheese sandwich. And that I'm dying of thirst. I already drank the pop I'd brought hours ago."

He waited for her to add she'd been pining for the sight of him, but she didn't. Fighting disappointment, he released her slowly.

Diane stepped back, turning to open the box. "What kind of pizza did you bring?"

"Pepperoni and black olive. I hope that's okay."

"Perfect." She inhaled deeply.

While he twisted the tops off the two bottles of beer she pulled up an extra chair. He handed her a beer. Let her eat first, and then he'd find out how much she *had* missed him, he decided, shoving aside his impatience and sitting in the straight-backed chair. He took the slice of pizza she handed him while he returned her smile.

For a few moments they were busy eating and didn't talk. Then Diane sat back with a satisfied sigh, patting her stomach. "That was great," she said. "I'm glad you came."

Adam drained his beer bottle. "I wasn't sure you would be."

Her brows lowered into a frown. "You weren't? But I told you I just had so much work here—" She indicated the books and papers she had shoved aside earlier. "You run a business, too. You must understand."

Adam tried to speak patiently. "I'm also involved in a fairly new relationship. You can't blame me for wondering if you were just trying to avoid me."

Embarrassed, Diane leapt to her feet and began to pace. Trust Adam to cut right to the heart of it. "I'm sorry you felt that way," she said defensively, "but you have to remember that my business comes before everything else."

Adam rose and stood in front of her. "That's a dangerous attitude," he said quietly. "Things happen, things beyond our control. Businesses fail. Then what do we have?"

Diane raised her hands as if to ward off his words. "Relationships fail, too," she said, remembering how Earl had dumped her. "There are no guarantees."

"True." Adam was watching her, a hint of stubbornness on his lean face. "All I want is to give us a chance. We could have something special together."

His words made Diane blush. Was she making too much of it? She was going to protest, but then she felt intense pleasure at the idea that he hadn't given up on them. Following close behind was the desire that Adam always stirred in her. She kept herself from swaying toward him, but something in her eyes must have given her away.

Adam's gaze became intent as his arms came around her and his head tilted closer. For a moment he searched her face. "I missed you," he muttered, and then his mouth covered hers.

Their lips clung, and she savored his warmth and power as his arms tightened. She had missed this, and no amount of work had succeeded in banishing it from her mind. When he lifted his mouth from hers, she slid her hands across his shoulders and urged him back to her.

This second kiss unleashed the passion his earlier embraces had only hinted at. He teased her lips apart and swept boldly inside, claiming her. His hands touched and grasped and caressed, making her body hum with desire as her senses filled with him. All Diane could do was to hang on, as she absorbed his heat and matched it with her own.

Adam tore his mouth from hers, dragging in a breath before burying his face into her shoulder. His hand tenderly covered her breast and his fingers shaped the tip into a rounded bead. His touch sent a shower of sparks bursting through Diane and she shifted, arching back to allow him greater access. As his teeth closed delicately on her earlobe, he began to unbutton her shirt.

Diane had been hovering on the very edge of desire, ready to topple over into a mindless sea of passion, but the last remnants of coherent thought brought her abruptly back to earth. She closed her eyes, willing herself back into that blissful state, but it was no use.

Her sudden tension had communicated itself to Adam, who stilled his hand and stepped back to study her silently. "I want you," he rasped, eyes dark with hunger. Then his chest heaved and his mouth twisted into a crooked grin. "But I'm rushing you, aren't I? And you're not ready." He took a tortured breath and re-buttoned her shirt with hands that trembled with the effort to find control, then squeezed her shoulder lightly before he let her go.

"I'm sorry." A part of Diane acknowledged that control, ragged as it might be. "I didn't mean to—" She gestured, at a loss to continue.

"Do you want to see me again?"

The question was a bald one, devoid of feeling, though Adam's face showed lines of strain.

Diane thought quickly. How simple it would be to tell him no. How simple and how impossible. Her mouth refused to form the words. Lies never came easy, even if they were ultimately for her own good.

Adam waited silently, his mouth a grim line, his body rigid. Diane felt badly that he should even have to ask such a question and she discarded the opportunity to back away.

"Yes," she said, touching his cheek with the tips of her fingers. "I would like to go on seeing you, if it's what you want, too."

Adam's laugh was almost a groan. "My feelings should be plain enough."

Diane tried to explain, knowing as she did that she was making excuses to both of them. "I've been so busy with work. It's nothing personal."

He sighed, relieved, as he leaned into the touch of her hand. "I guess that's all I need to know for now." He dropped a hard kiss onto her mouth. "And I hope you'll find more time for us."

"I'll try."

Adam's tone was suddenly earnest. "Try hard."

"Just because you don't care about success, don't expect me to be the same way," she cautioned him.

Adam's expression darkened, a chill settling over his masculine features. "Maybe I understand success and ruthless ambition all too well."

"I can't believe that," she said, stung by his tone. "You've made it so easily that you don't have a clue how hard some of us have had to work, to sacrifice, just to get this far."

As she took a breath, he cut her off. The pain on his face made her step back. His eyes were full of something terrible as they bored into her. "Lady," he ground out, "I know more about ambition than you can ever hope to. If you're smart, you'll *pray* you never learn what I've learned the hard way."

He turned from her, his shoulders slumped. Diane wanted to touch him, to comfort him somehow, but when she reached out, he jerked away.

"I think it's time I left," he said in a hollow tone. Someday he might have to try to convince her, but not tonight. His emotions were too close to the surface, and he might end up saying something he couldn't take back. Better to retreat while he still had some control left. He bundled up the empty pizza box. "You undoubtedly have things to finish up here."

"A little." If she had questions, she was holding them in.

There was nothing left to say, so after making sure she would be all right alone, he left her to finish her paperwork. On the way back to his apartment, he wondered if he should have just kept his mouth shut. Sexual frustration was no excuse to say things she wasn't ready to hear, and he wasn't ready to explain. He had to get his own feelings in order before he could hope to make sense out of what was going on between the two of them.

"I SHOULD BE BACK in an hour and a half," Diane told Carol as she took the last of her afternoon deliveries out the door and loaded them into the van.

"Did you call your sister back?" Carol asked.

Diane shook her head. "Forgot. If she calls again, find out what she wants, will you?"

Carol shrugged. "Okay, but I'm sure she'd rather talk to you than me. You're lucky to have your family close, you know, but you take them for granted."

Diane shook off her feelings of guilt. They had to understand how busy she was. "I'll have more time when business is steady," she told Carol. "They understand that."

For a moment, Carol looked as though she meant to say more. Having lost her own mother to cancer when she'd been in high school, she was overly sensitive to the situation. "Okay," she said after a moment. "See you." She went back to the flowers she had been arranging as Diane let the door swing shut behind her.

Pulling out onto the street, Diane glanced around, glad to be outside. It was a beautiful day—the sky an incredible shade of blue, the air warm with the promise of summer. Beside her on the seat was a clipboard filled with orders. What more could a hardworking businessperson ask for?

Diane quickly closed her mind to the flood of possibilities that rose. Wasn't it enough that she had a full load to deliver? Slowly, steadily, business at Diane's Flowers was growing. People knew they could count on her, even at the last minute. She was working harder than ever, afraid to let up for even a day. If she relaxed, everything she had worked so hard for might come crashing down around her. She had seen it happen to others.

On the other hand, if she didn't find more time for Adam, might he lose patience and disappear from her life just as Earl had? The dilemma was a tough one—weighing what she had always wanted against what she wanted more each day, success against love, and wishing she could have both.

Why didn't men ever have to face such dilemmas?

Just that morning Adam, having decided to quit work early, called and asked her to share a picnic in the hills. If only he took his responsibilities more seriously, the ensuing argument would never have happened. While Adam turned down work, Diane was busy hustling every wedding and funeral she could, finding his attitude as incomprehensible as she suspected hers was to him.

She pulled over to the curb, checking an address. After delivering a birthday bouquet of red and white carnations to a delighted senior citizen, she climbed back into the pink van and headed for the next stop, her thoughts veering back to Adam before she reached the corner. What had he meant when he told her he knew more about ambition than he hoped she ever would? He had sounded so bitter.

She pulled up to the main door of the local hospital to deliver five orders, a marked increase over the week before. While she set up a collapsible delivery cart, a family came bursting out the front door, parents in careful attendance of a small girl with her arm in a cast while two other siblings pranced close by. They all wore clean but shabby clothing and the homey group made Diane think of her own family as she unloaded the van.

There had never been any extra money when she was growing up, and often not enough for necessities either. For that Diane had always blamed her father, who had been content to stay with the same low-paying job until he retired. *It will never happen to me,* she vowed, loading the cart. But she didn't want to lose Adam, either.

Adam, whose touch was the sweetest thing she had ever experienced, who could make her head swim with a kiss.

Blinking away the daydream, Diane stepped off the elevator inside the hospital and glanced around with confusion. She was on the wrong floor. Grumbling, she turned and pushed the button again, tapping her foot with impatience. This was getting her nowhere. Greeting one of the nurses she had come to know by sight, she got back on the elevator, pulling the cart behind her.

"NICE DAY FOR A RIDE!" An old man in his old car waved to Adam, slowing to pass his bicycle on the narrow country road. Adam waved back.

It would have been even nicer if he weren't alone. Perhaps if Adam wasn't so hung up on a certain workaholic who didn't believe in playing hooky he wouldn't be taking this solitary bike ride along the river road.

It occurred to him that this sense of rejection was how Penny must have felt when, day after day, evening after evening, he had chosen his business in L.A. over her companionship. No wonder she had finally looked elsewhere. It was a damned painful feeling. Perhaps she had even known what it had taken him three years of marriage to understand—that he didn't love her as a husband should. Once the passion between them had started to cool, there wasn't much left. And that was one more reason for him to feel guilty. Perhaps he wasn't even capable of real love.

Even six months before, Adam wouldn't have believed that he would find himself in such a position, his sense of well-being so heavily influenced by a woman. Since Penny's death he had managed to avoid emotional entanglements, but now he was beginning to feel as if he had been frozen and was just starting to thaw. So far the return of feeling was as uncomfortable as the prick of sharp needles.

The sun beat down as he pedaled silently. A breeze off the water kept him from being uncomfortably hot but he could feel dampness on the back of his tank top beneath the pack he wore, and his throat was dry.

Another car passed him, horn blaring as it swept by uncomfortably close. Not all drivers were courteous to bicyclists, one of the reasons Adam wore a helmet when he rode.

He decided to stop by his sister's house and eat his lunch there. If she wasn't home he could still sit by her duck pond, in the shade of an ancient willow tree.

Lori's car was parked in the long driveway that ran past the old farmhouse where she lived with Tom. Adam dismounted and walked his bike toward the front door, along the border of bright pink petunias he had helped her plant. Lori worked as a billing clerk at the hospital, but today was her day off. Adam suspected that he would find her working in the yard or completing some project on the house she shared with her new husband.

"Come in, bro," she said in response to his knock at her screen door. "I was just taking a break from the vegetable garden. Want some lemonade?"

Adam shrugged out of his pack and took off his helmet. "Okay if I eat my lunch while I'm here?"

"Sure. I'd like the company."

He followed her into the large kitchen that was the hub of the house Tom had started to remodel even before he met Lori. Adam perched on a white bar stool topped by a red and white checkered cushion that matched the café curtains, while she poured lemonade from a pitcher.

"Why aren't you working today?" Lori asked as she handed him a glass.

Adam had pulled his lunch from the pack and unwrapped the cold meat loaf sandwich, taking a hungry bite.

"Are things slow at the shop?" she demanded before he could reply.

Adam glared at her while he washed down the mouthful with lemonade. "I can't believe how many people are interested in my business and how I'm running it."

Lori's eyes, dark like his, flooded with hurt. "I'm sorry," she said quickly.

"No," Adam corrected, rising to give her a quick hug. "I'm the one who's sorry. Sorry that I'm so touchy."

Lori held on to his arms, studying his face. "What's going on?" she asked softly, inviting his confidence.

Adam pulled away, raking his hair back as he leaned against the white-tiled counter, taking another long drink before he answered.

"Do you think I'm a goof-off?" he demanded.

Lori's puzzled expression deepened. "A goof-off?" she echoed. "Of course not. What brought that on?"

Adam shook his head. "Damned if I know. My business is doing just fine, but lately I've begun to wonder if that's enough. I left L.A. to avoid the rat race, but maybe I've gone too far the other way." He finished the first sandwich half in another big bite.

"You left with good reason," she said encouragingly. "In Los Angeles your business was your whole life."

"And it cost Penny hers," he said bitterly.

Immediately Lori shook a finger at him. "You have to stop blaming yourself for that," she scolded. "Anyway, what's all this talk about being a lazy old worm, anyway?"

Her words made Adam smile, as they were meant to. "I wouldn't go that far. I've just been wondering lately if my attitude is out of line." He rewrapped the other sandwich half and stuffed it into the pouch, suddenly restless. Then he finished his lemonade in a long swallow.

"If it ain't broke, don't fix it, right?" he asked, glancing at the back door.

Lori followed the direction of his gaze. "I'm glad we worked out whatever it was we did," she said. "Maybe one of these days, you'll explain what's going on."

"Maybe."

"Meanwhile, don't rush off. We can talk about something more mundane." She grinned.

Adam returned her smile and sat back down. "I can stick around a little longer."

"Good. That'll give me an excuse not to have to go back and work in the garden for a while."

"Right. Is everything okay with you?"

The expression on her face answered his question. It was obvious she was happy. "Wonderful."

"I'm glad to hear it. Tom's a pretty good guy."

"Yes, he is." Her dark eyes twinkled, then she went to the fridge and poured him another glass of lemonade while they talked of inconsequential things, and people they both knew. After a while, Adam glanced at the wall clock and rose reluctantly.

"I guess you'll have to go back to work," he said, draining his glass. "I'd better get moving." He wanted to ride farther before he had to turn back toward town.

"Before you run off, how about finding a date and joining Tom and me for dinner a week from this Friday?" Lori asked. "It's his birthday and we're going to that new place out on the highway, the one with the great steaks and the live music."

Adam thought of Diane and how surprised Lori would be to see her again. "I'll let you know in a couple of days," he said, pushing open the screen door. "Okay?"

"Sure. Thanks for stopping by."

She looked as if there was more she would have liked to ask, but Adam ignored it as he smiled at her through the screen. "Thanks for the lemonade," he said, strapping his pack and helmet back on before picking up his bike. As he rode back down the long driveway, he found himself looking forward to showing Diane off to Tom and Lori. If she agreed to see him that evening.

5

"DINNER WITH LORI and Tom sounds like fun," Diane said in answer to Adam's invitation as they rested at the edge of the pool behind his apartment building. It was Sunday, and she had managed to rush through her chores in time to join him for a swim and a barbecue at his place. "It will be nice to see them again." She remembered the wedding where she had danced with Adam. It would be interesting to find out if Tom and Lori still had that special newlywed glow. The thought of dancing with Adam again wasn't hard to take, either.

"How about one more race before we get out?" he asked, his eyes gleaming as they strayed to the bodice of Diane's one-piece suit. "Then I'd better start the charcoal if we want to eat anytime soon."

Diane grinned and pushed her wet hair off her forehead as she nodded. "I'll get you this time," she threatened.

"Never happen," Adam taunted, watching with interest as her violet eyes narrowed and she thrust her chin out. Her hands tensed against the edge of the pool. "Ready?" she asked, then immediately pushed off. Adam was right behind her.

This time, instead of swimming past her as he had managed to do in their last three races, he hooked an arm around her waist when he came abreast of her. Diane struggled as they both went under. Before they broke the surface again, he cupped her chin in one hand and kissed her. They came up together, legs tangled intimately, mouths touching, Diane's hands resting on his shoulders. Adam released her reluctantly and they both took in some air.

"No fair," she said, laughing. "I was ahead."

He dropped another kiss onto her cool lips. "I'd say we both won."

"You may be right." Before he had time to prepare himself, Diane shifted her hands to his head and ducked him, at the same time propelling herself away. When Adam surfaced, sputtering, she was almost to the edge of the pool. Grinning, he followed, pausing when he got there to watch her emerge.

Diane's swimsuit, a deep purple lycra that almost matched her eyes, was extremely sexy in its simplicity. The legs were high-cut, lengthening her shapely thighs. The plain fabric clung to her slim body and outlined the soft swell of her breasts, dipping between them in an alluring *V*.

While Adam gazed up at her, Diane straightened and grabbed her towel. Patting her dripping hair, she turned to look down at him. "Going to stay in all day?" she teased.

"I may," Adam drawled. He loved her lighthearted smile and the way she had been laughing as they played in the water. It struck him that they both needed times like this together more often, away from the pressures of work that kept them apart. As he climbed out of the water, he hoped Diane felt the same way.

They changed back into dry clothes before they ate, and afterward Diane helped him clean up and wash the dishes. All afternoon Adam had been trying—without much success—to keep his thoughts away from how he hoped the evening would end.

Now the end of the evening was almost here.

Diane rinsed the last dish and set it in the drainer as Adam wiped off the counter.

"You're a terrific cook," she said, smiling. "That meal was wonderful."

Adam had served the steaks with baked potatoes from the microwave and a salad he had prepared earlier. Now he took the washcloth from Diane and tossed it into the sink. His arms came around her and he stared deep into her eyes.

"The day's not over," he murmured, leaning closer.

For a timeless moment, Diane relaxed in his arms, returning his kiss with interest. Adam's body responded immediately, hardening against her.

"You feel good," he whispered, stringing kisses along her jaw before he returned to her parted lips. When he finally looked at Diane, her eyes were clouded with desire and she clung to him. He couldn't resist rubbing his hips against hers, letting her feel the strength of his desire.

She moaned, fueling the passion that threatened to overtake him.

He gathered her closer and kissed her again, tracing the sensitive tissue of her lips with the tip of his tongue, slipping into her mouth when a tremor shook her. How sweetly she responded, making his blood simmer and his nerves dance. He broke the heated kiss and buried his face in her hair, his breathing rapid and shallow. Diane made him forget everything he had ever learned about control and patience.

Her hands tightened at his waist, her breasts were pushed against his chest, and another hungry little sound worked its way past her lips. Adam's senses spun and he dragged in the faintly flowery scent that rose from her hair and her warm skin. He lifted his head, staring intently into her face, absently noticing her thick, curling lashes and the freckles scattered across her nose. Diane's eyes fluttered open and locked with his. They widened and after a long moment she looked hastily away.

"I can't."

Adam, who had been about to scoop her into his arms, went still. "Why not? You want me, too. I know you do. What's stopping us?" His voice sounded raw and scratchy, even to him.

Diane pulled out of his embrace and moved to the window, hugging her arms around herself as if she'd felt a sudden chill. Diane turned. "I'm not sure I'm ready yet." She watched his expressive face. First tension and then puzzlement flashed across it. She came closer to him and raised a hand to caress his cheek.

"I shouldn't have let things go on so long," she said. "But kissing you . . ." Her voice trailed off and the way she smiled made him ache.

It was all he could do not to grab her.

"My life has been so hectic lately," she said apologetically. "And I don't want to make any mistakes."

"We're not a mistake," he said, realizing he really meant it. He took her hand and raised it to his mouth, his lips whispering across her knuckles with the lightest of kisses as his dark eyes watched her face.

"What makes you so sure we aren't a mistake?" Diane asked, her hand trembling in his.

"We feel right together," he said, trying to put his feelings into words. "There's something very special going on when I touch you, when I kiss you. Something I want to explore further, something I haven't found before, with anyone." Something that should send him running hell-bent for the hills, a voice inside him whispered.

"I know you feel it, too," he continued, slipping his arms around her. "I can tell."

"Yes," she admitted. "I do."

When he kissed her again, she kissed him back, her mouth melting hotly into his, her body pressing tight against him, telling him in no uncertain terms that she had changed her mind. In a mere instant of time, Adam's control was in shreds as the heat rose between them.

Lifting his head, he looked into her deep, inviting eyes. "Are you sure?" His breath caught painfully as he waited for her answer.

Instead of speaking, Diane pulled his head back down to hers. He was right, there was something special between them, something she wanted to hang on to. Maybe it was time to allow herself to feel, to dream, just a little. As long as she kept it under control.

Her restraint was abruptly shattered as Adam slid one hand under the loose hem of her blouse and up to cover her breast, his thumb flicking over the nipple beneath the sheer whisper of nylon and lace. With a moan, Diane tightened her hands around his neck, burying her fingers in his hair.

"Shall I protect you?" Adam asked, gazing down at her with a tender smile. "I can, you know."

Diane shook her head. "No need. I took care of it."

He bent and scooped her into his arms, settling on the wide leather couch with her cradled in his lap. Quickly they shed their clothes, the fierce heat of desire urging them on.

As they lay side by side, Diane let her wandering hands explore Adam's broad chest and the pattern of hair that swirled downward, as he concentrated his attention on her breasts, caressing and then kissing them until the tips were tight and straining.

As Diane's fingers hesitated on the warm skin of his lean hips, Adam sucked in a breath and urged her legs apart with one knee.

"You're beautiful," he muttered, sliding a hairy thigh between her smooth ones. "I'd suspected that you were gorgeous, but the reality puts my imagination to shame." His hand caressed her rounded buttocks and then his fingers traced the crease between them. His other hand drifted into the curls below her stomach, probing gently. When Diane uttered a broken cry, he kissed her hotly, muffling the sound.

Unable to wait a moment longer, Diane opened to him more fully, her hands tightening on his hips as she murmured little sounds of encouragement. When Adam slid into her, she wrapped her legs around him, holding him close, arching into his power and heat, until they both found release seconds away from each other.

Long moments followed as Adam shifted back to her side and then slid his arms around her soft body to hold her close.

"Mmm," he said when he could breathe again. "I told you we had something special."

Diane couldn't help but agree with him, enjoying his closeness as they both recovered their strength. After a few moments of lying together, murmuring quietly, she began to shift restlessly.

Adam's dark eyes probed hers. "Second thoughts?"

"No." She touched his cheek tenderly. "I just have some sorting out to do."

He frowned. "Anything I need to be concerned about?"

Diane smiled and reached up to kiss him lightly. "No," she repeated, "I just wasn't expecting anything that—" She gestured with her hand.

"That wonderful," he finished for her.

"Yes." Her gaze slid away from his. "I really had better go," she said. "I have paperwork to finish."

"I'm jealous," Adam confessed, stroking her shoulder with his fingers. "I feel like I'm competing with your business."

Diane almost denied what he said, but then she hesitated. If she were honest, at least with herself, she couldn't say for sure if he was wrong. Her feelings were too mixed up.

She compromised. "I wish you wouldn't say that." The hesitation on his face caught at her heart. "You're important to me," she admitted softly. "You must realize that now."

His brow furrowed.

"I've already told you that nothing comes in the way of my business," she added a little defensively. "Don't try to make me feel guilty."

Adam's frown deepened and he ran a hand over his face. "You aren't telling me anything I don't already know about ambition," he said finally. "I've been there myself, and maybe I should tell you why I feel the way I do."

All thoughts of rushing back to work fled when Diane heard the pain in Adam's voice. She started raising a hand to touch him, then thought better of it. "Perhaps you should."

He sat back, turning her so he could see her face. She was impatient to hear what he had to say.

Adam looked away, as if he were gathering his thoughts. Then he gazed searchingly into her eyes.

"I grew up in L.A.," he said. "You knew that."

Diane nodded.

"My father's a successful surgeon there. He always wanted me to be a doctor, too."

Diane remained silent, afraid to interrupt his train of thought. No wonder their attitudes were so different. He had grown up in an affluent home, taking the things she had gone without much more for granted.

Adam pushed back his untidy hair, which was mussed from their lovemaking. "I think Dad had planned on me joining his practice, but instead I dropped out of college and went to vocational school. I'd thought about it a lot before I went ahead. Then after I'd worked in a body shop for a while, I borrowed some money from Dad and opened my own place. When business picked up, I got married to the girl I'd been dating since high school."

Diane felt a burning surge of jealousy toward the woman who had shared his life so intimately. "What happened?" she couldn't keep from asking. Was he divorced?

"I wanted to show my father that I'd made the right choice so I worked hard to be a success. Things were going pretty well. Then I met a guy who was on a hit television series at the time." He mentioned a show that Diane used to watch. "He'd seen my work, and he had an old Porsche he wanted redone. I did a good job, hoping that maybe he'd recommend me to his friends. He did." Adam paused, smiling wryly. "In a few months I had more business than I could handle. I even did a couple of custom cars for a movie, *Teen Surfers' Beach Party*."

His expression was questioning.

"I must have missed that one," Diane admitted.

He shrugged, running a hand across his chin. "Anyway, I moved the business to bigger quarters and hired more help. I still worked a lot of hours. I couldn't trust anyone else to do the quality of work I wanted done." His eyes narrowed but Diane refused to read any significance there, returning his knowing look with a bland one of her own.

"Then what happened?" She wanted to know about his marriage.

"The money was rolling in, and I was busier than ever."

He stopped and swallowed. Diane could see the shadows in his eyes. For some reason it was painful for Adam to recall this part of his life.

"Your father must have been proud of you," she said, to keep him talking.

"Well, he understood hard work. He's done it all his life." He sighed. "Anyway, pretty soon Penny and I were being invited to a lot of parties. I, of course, was too busy working, so after a while Penny got sick of waiting for me to come home and started going by herself." Adam looked away again, jaw knotted. "She wanted to have a baby, but I wasn't ready. She wanted to buy a house, but I didn't have time to go with her and look for one."

His voice had risen and Diane thought she was beginning to understand the load of guilt he carried.

"I didn't even notice when she started running with a new crowd," he continued. "By then we were fighting all the time, about everything. I was too busy with work to see when she started using drugs. And then she overdosed."

The baldness of his words made Diane gasp as he leaned forward, putting his head into his hands. "That got my attention, but it was too late. Penny was dead."

For a moment Diane was too shocked to move. Then she began to rub one hand gently across his rigid shoulders. "I'm sorry," she said, feeling inadequate. Did he still love his wife? "But it wasn't your fault, and it doesn't make all ambition bad. You were trying to build a future for the two of you."

Adam moved away from her touch. "I sold the business and moved here, away from the roller coaster ride, away from temptation. Now I work as much as necessary, but I don't let it consume me. It isn't my whole life. Do you understand?" His expression was fierce.

Diane wasn't sure what he was getting at. "I think so."

Adam groaned, shaking his head. "Don't end up like I did," he told her. "Stop and smell those flowers you're selling. Enjoy life. Don't get caught up in the race for money and success. Believe me, it can be a very hollow victory when you do succeed. And then at some point you realize that you have nothing else."

Diane took a deep breath. "That won't happen to me." She waited until he looked at her. "Adam, I'm not you. All my life I had to do with less than other kids had, missing out because we didn't have the money. And not just extras, either. I'm talking about clothes from the secondhand store, barely enough food, rental housing you couldn't imagine. To my dad, security meant not changing jobs, no matter what. He had no sick pay for when he was ill. He was passed over for promotion time and again, at the mercy of the bosses who stole his ideas and took credit for his work. All because he was afraid to take a chance. That isn't going to happen to me, and I'm not going to slow down and then realize someday that I've lost my will to win, that I've settled for less than I deserve."

Adam remained silent.

Diane cast about for something reassuring she could tell him. "I will promise to be more organized, though. I'll see what I can do to avoid working so many hours, okay?"

Adam wasn't smiling when he leaned over to place a kiss on her upturned mouth. For a moment, warmth flooded her.

"How about hiring another employee?" he suggested, surprising her. Obviously he'd been giving the subject some thought. "Then that person or Carol could do the deliveries while you handle making the arrangements and keeping up the books. Wouldn't that help?"

She frowned. "I don't know if I can afford someone else and Carol doesn't want to work any more hours, but I'll think about it."

For a moment he looked as though he was going to argue. Then his expression softened. "Okay. That's fair enough."

Diane touched his arm. "I'm sorry about Penny," she said, "but I'm glad you told me." Perhaps she would be able to understand Adam better now. At least he had a reason for his apparent lack of ambition.

He slid an arm across her shoulders. "Can you stay with me tonight?"

Needing to be alone with her thoughts about the tumultuous experience she'd just shared with him, Diane shook her head. "I'd better go home."

To her mingled relief and disappointment, Adam didn't argue. Instead he rose to pick up her scattered clothing. Ignoring his own nakedness, he began to dress her, stopping often to kiss a patch of skin before covering it or tell her how attractive she was to him. By the time Diane was clad in everything but her shoes, he raised his hands.

"You'd better finish dressing yourself," he said, smiling ruefully, "or I'm afraid I'll be taking it all off again."

Diane felt her cheeks glow with warmth as she zipped her jeans and slid into her sandals. She wasn't sure what to say.

"Just think about what I told you, okay?" Adam said as he was donning his own clothes.

"Okay. I'm glad we talked," she said softly. She had an idea that telling her about the past had cost him a lot.

"Yeah. Me, too. Don't wait too long to hire someone," he said. "You're working yourself into the ground."

After a brief hesitation, Diane lifted her face and kissed him on the cheek. It wasn't easy to go.

"Good luck with your paperwork," Adam said rather dryly as she picked up her purse.

"Thanks for understanding."

As he walked her to her car, he almost confessed how much he hated to let her go. Instead he said, "I'll call you," as he handed her the tote with her wet swimsuit and towel inside. "And don't forget our dinner with Lori and Tom on Friday."

"Friday?" For a moment Diane went blank. "Oh, that's right. I'm looking forward to seeing them again." She stopped by the driver's door. "I had a lovely time."

Adam's eyes darkened. "Me, too, special lady." He dropped a kiss on her nose, knowing he was going to miss her like crazy until they saw each other again. He ran his fingers lightly down her arm.

Diane stepped back as Adam opened the car door, severely tempted to change her mind and go back up the steps with him. Already she missed having his strong arms around her, the touch of his mouth heating hers as he took her to paradise. Keeping her mind off him while she did paperwork was going to be difficult, if not impossible.

ALL THAT WEEK, though Diane only talked to Adam once briefly, single daisies tied with ribbon began showing up in the oddest places—on her doorstep, the seat of her van, in her mailbox. Once there was one waiting for her on the desk in her office when she got back from making deliveries. Carol claimed to have no knowledge of it. But even though the back door had been unlocked, Diane wasn't sure she believed her. The daisies weren't the kind they carried, either. The flowers were bigger, the petals a single rather than a double row. The ribbon was a color of deep blue violet they didn't have in stock.

Sitting in her battered steno chair, Diane twirled the last offering between her palms, watching the white petals spin like the spokes of a wheel. Remembering a game she and her sisters played as children, she began to pluck the petals one by one.

"Loves me, loves me not," she recited under her breath. "Loves me," another petal pulled, "loves me not." She dropped them in her lap, fingers reaching for another. "Loves me—"

"I remember doing that." Carol's voice from the doorway made Diane jump as the denuded blossom fell from her fingers.

"I was just—" Carol's grin stopped her words.

"You're a florist," she said. "I'm assuming that you're just testing the competition's goods."

"Yeah," Diane answered. "Just testing." Her cheeks were warm with embarrassment.

"I'd give up a lunch hour to hear how it came out," Carol said, going back out the door. Behind her, Diane scooped the daisy and loose petals into the wastebasket before she turned her attention to the journal, wondering, too, how it would have come out.

Each time she found one of the saucy old-fashioned flowers it reminded her of Adam and the special time they'd shared—and she couldn't banish certain erotic thoughts from her mind.

When Friday finally rolled around after a hellishly busy week, Diane found her glance darting constantly to the phone at work and then veering away, while preparing one of the elaborate arrangements for a wedding that evening. Luckily it was scheduled to begin later than normal or she would have been in real trouble.

Where had the day gone? Diane was supposed to have had enough time to finish this order, leave work at five and change for dinner. Now, thanks to a broken-down delivery truck that hadn't brought the special-ordered flowers, Diane had been forced to make the long trip into Sacramento to pick them up herself, a task that had decimated her schedule.

As if that wasn't enough, Carol had been complaining about not feeling well. Diane was worried about her normally hardworking assistant and, if she could, would have sent Carol home to bed.

There was no help for it; Diane would have to cancel another date or at least postpone it for several hours, and hope that Adam would understand. Again. She had been working up her nerve to call him for an hour. Glancing at her watch, she knew she could put it off no longer. Neither could she give him the news over the phone.

"Feeling any better?" she asked Carol hopefully.

She shook her head. "Worse. But I think I can hang on."

"I appreciate it," Diane said. "If you can manage alone, I'll be back in a few minutes. There's something I have to do."

Carol, who had just begun working on a bridesmaid's bouquet of lavender roses and baby's breath, nodded wearily.

After eyeing her friend with concern, Diane hurried to the back room to apply lip gloss and collect her purse. She owed it to Adam to give him the news in person.

She found him sanding a car that had been freshly primered in a dull gray. The boy who worked for him part-time wasn't around, and for that Diane was grateful.

"I can't believe this!" Adam shouted when she told him. His face was dark with anger, thick brows knotted together as he towered over her in his baggy coveralls. Even in the dirty work clothes, with a smudge down one cheek, he managed to look sexy. "You know that my sister and her husband are expecting us this evening," he went on, pacing. "It's Tom's birthday and too late for them to make other dinner plans."

Diane twisted the strap of her purse in her hands, at a loss what to say. She had known he would be disappointed, but hoped he would be more understanding.

"I'm sorry," she said anxiously. "I wouldn't do this if I had a choice, but I don't. Those arrangements have to be finished and delivered tonight. It's not my fault."

His frown deepened. He was angrier than she had ever seen him. "A lot has been coming up lately," he growled. "You're a florist, not an obstetrician."

"What does that mean?" Diane drew herself up to her full height, offended by his tone.

"It's not a baby you're delivering, after all."

"I know that, but it's still important to the people who hired me. They can't have a wedding without flowers! I wish the delivery truck hadn't broken down, but it did, and I had to pick up the special order myself and now I have to get all the bouquets and arrangements set up and delivered for the Martin-Shindler wedding and there's nothing I can do about it." Diane felt like crying. "I'm sorry!" she repeated, blinking back tears of frustration, "but they have to have their flowers."

"*Sorry* doesn't help much," Adam snapped. "I thought I was beginning to mean something to you." Perhaps he was being unreasonable, but she always had an excuse and he was starting to feel totally expendable, despite the intimacy they had shared.

"You do mean something to me! It's not my fault that your business isn't important to you. Mine is!" Diane realized what she had just said and bit her lip. It was no time to be making comparisons.

If anything, Adam's expression became even more forbidding. He tossed aside the purple rag he'd been using to clean his hands. "If you cared at all, you'd find time for me in your life. I make the time for you." With a sound of disgust, he turned away as Diane watched him anxiously, at a loss for what to say without making things worse.

The silence stretched tensely, then he looked back at her, eyes opaque. "You're probably right," he said softly, surprising her. "Maybe I just expect too much."

Diane waited but he didn't say anything else, and she couldn't read his face. After apologizing once more for canceling their dinner date, she left him standing there and hurried back to her shop. Thank goodness that Carol was staying to help.

When Diane got back, Carol greeted her with a pale face and a groan.

"I'm glad you're here. I hate to do this to you, but I really feel just awful. I think I've caught that bug my daughter brought home from school." Carol was a single parent. She had never been married to her daughter's father, but he helped her financially so she only had to work part-time and could be home a lot until Melissa started school.

Diane touched her hand to Carol's brow, which felt distinctly clammy. "Go home," she said, hiding her dismay. "I can manage alone."

Carol didn't even argue. She grabbed her purse and headed for the door. "Thanks. I hope I'm over this soon."

"Me, too," Diane muttered, thinking that Saturday would be an unbelievably hectic day if Carol wasn't better. Diane would have to lock up while she delivered orders, and hope that anyone who encountered the answering machine would leave a message or call back. In the meantime, she had a large order to finish.

She had just sat down with more flowers when the phone rang. Grumbling, she got up to answer it. The best she could hope for was that Carol's flu was of the short-term variety.

BY THE MIDDLE of the following week, Diane was tearing her hair. Carol had been calling in sick every morning, telling Diane how much she wished she'd get better so she could return to work, and Diane had been putting in fourteen-hour days trying to keep up. Adam's suggestion that she hire another employee came back to haunt her, but she was too busy to do anything about it.

On this particular afternoon Diane was putting together a bouquet of alstramaria, a lavender flower that resembled a small orchid. It came from Holland and was a very popular addition to arrangements. She imported a lot of her flowers from Europe and South America, and potted plants from Canada.

The front door to the shop opened, the bell above it tinkling cheerily. Diane wanted to scream with frustration, but instead she managed a welcoming smile.

An older woman with gray hair and an ample build came toward the worktable where Diane was seated. "Are you Diane Simmons?"

"Yes." It was unusual for customers to ask for her by her full name. "How can I help you?"

"I hope that I can help you," the woman said, glancing around. "Adam sent me. I'm his sister's neighbor, Marilyn Pringle."

Diane rose and shook the hand she extended. "Nice to meet you."

"Adam said you might be in the market for some help," Marilyn said, looking around again. "This is a real nice place."

"Thank you," Diane said automatically, "but I'd need someone with experience. I wouldn't have time to train you."

Marilyn's smile widened. "I understand. I had my own business, Pringle's Posies, here in town for twenty years before I retired."

"Really?" Diane asked, suddenly very interested. "Of course I've heard of it. But why would you want to go back to work for someone else?"

"I'm bored," Marilyn confessed. "My kids are grown, my husband's gone to work all day, and I miss keeping busy. I could come in just about whatever hours you wanted."

Diane needed no further urging. "When can you start?"

Marilyn unbuttoned the cuffs of her striped shirt and rolled up the sleeves. "How about now?"

SEVERAL DAYS LATER, over a lunch that she had instigated, Diane was able to thank Adam for sending Marilyn to her. He had been cool when she called to invite him, but he hadn't turned her down. Once they were face-to-face, he'd thawed quickly after telling her she had missed a great evening. Diane hadn't asked if he had taken someone else and he didn't volunteer the information. It probably served her right if he had.

"Marilyn's a wonder," Diane replied to Adam's question. "Even with Carol back, I can't remember how I got along without her. She knows everything about the business."

Adam reached across the table and squeezed her hand. "Seeing you more often is all the thanks I need."

Diane flushed and glanced at her watch. "I'd better go. We stagger our lunch hours. Marilyn's there alone

and I want to make sure she does the accounts right."
Diane was still nervous about delegating so much of the
work, but it was nice to get away for a little while without feeling guilty.

Adam frowned at the apparent contradiction between Marilyn's capability and Diane's willingness to
let her work on her own, but didn't say anything as he
rose and pulled back her chair. He hoped that she would
learn to trust Marilyn and not double-check everything the older woman did, or her help would be minimal. "I'll see you later, then. Around seven, okay?"

Diane agreed and left the small café after a quick kiss.
Adam followed her out more slowly. While he was
driving back to work, he passed a fish market. Thinking about Diane's cat and the hostile way it had greeted
him, he made a U-turn. Punkin was going to be his
friend, whether the shaggy orange feline wanted it or
not.

AT SEVEN O'CLOCK Diane was ready. They had decided
that Adam would bring a rented movie, and she was to
furnish beer and popcorn. An early evening in was
what they both needed during the busy work week.
Secretly Diane almost hoped they wouldn't have to
watch the movie. There were other pleasant ways to fill
the time. Since they had been together, she found herself wanting him again with a hunger that surprised her.
Her natural caution was being swept away, and along
with it her doubts. Remembering the feel of Adam's
mouth on hers and the way the touch of his big hands
made her tremble, Diane suppressed a wave of longing. How had she gotten along before he had transformed her life?

The doorbell rang and she glanced into the mirror, smoothing her hair and straightening the collar of the madras shirt she wore with matching shorts. Even though the day had been unseasonably cloudy, the air outside was heavy and warm, her apartment only slightly cooler.

"Mmm, I missed you," she exclaimed after she had opened the door, lifting her face for Adam's kiss. He hooked his free arm around her waist and held her close, nuzzling her neck before he claimed her lips.

"I like the idea of looking forward to seeing you after work," he said. "It brightens my day."

Diane's cheeks warmed, and she wasn't sure what to say. "What movie did you rent?"

"I'm sorry, but by the time I got to the video store, all the new releases were gone. I had to settle for one of the James Bond movies, but I don't remember which."

Diane shrugged. "That's okay. We can always talk if it gets too boring."

Adam's eyes gleamed. "That's what I thought, too."

For the first time, she noticed that he was carrying two packages. And one had a distinct aroma.

"What have you got?" she asked. "Bait?"

He grinned, opening the bag. "I guess you could call it that. Where's your cat?"

Diane glanced around. "I thought I saw him slink into the kitchen when I opened the door. Why?"

His grin widened. "I brought along something to convince him that I'm not really such a bad guy. Watch."

Diane followed Adam into the kitchen, where he withdrew a white-wrapped parcel from the bag. "Got some newspaper?"

She glanced around, then got out a paper towel. "Will this do?"

He nodded.

"What did you bring?"

"Some raw halibut. The butcher even cut it into slivers for me." He glanced around, spotting Punkin on a kitchen chair. The cat was ducked down, gold eyes boring into him. "He'll love this."

"Here, kitty," Adam called.

Punkin didn't move. He didn't even blink.

Feeling sorry for Adam, Diane called Punkin herself. At the sound of her voice, he jumped down and came slowly over, circling Adam wide and then purring as he rubbed against Diane's bare leg.

"Now give it to him," she said.

Adam took some of the fish from the package. "Here, kitty," he said again.

Diane watched Punkin, whose eyes had narrowed, as if he questioned the validity of Adam's bribe.

Adam extended his hand but Punkin didn't move. After a moment Adam carefully set down the treat on the paper towel between them. Both he and Diane waited silently while the big orange cat sniffed curiously. After a moment, Punkin came closer, and Adam gave Diane a triumphant grin.

Punkin investigated the offering thoroughly while Diane waited, scarcely breathing. Then the cat let them both know what he thought of Adam's gift.

6

"OH, NO," Diane groaned.

Punkin had turned his back on the fish, and was making scraping motions on the floor all around it with a front paw, as if he were doing his best to cover up something offensive. Then he cast a disdainful glance over his shoulder at Adam and stalked away, tail upright and quivering as if he had been mortally insulted.

As the silence lengthened, Diane picked up the paper towel and tried her best not to laugh. She wasn't sure which had been more comical—Punkin's pantomime or the stunned expression on Adam's face. Reaching for the package he still held, she said, "I guess he's not susceptible to bribes. Shall I put this in the fridge?"

For a moment Adam gazed at her blankly, then he shook his head, taking the crumpled paper towel from her fingers. "I'll put it in the dumpster," he said. "No point in smelling things up."

"Okay." Diane bit her lip, reminding herself that his feelings had been hurt. It took a real effort to keep the smile from forming when she remembered the way Punkin had "buried" Adam's offering, the gesture more eloquent than words.

While she was waiting for him to return from the dumpster, she searched for the cat, finding him perched on her bed, determinedly washing his paws.

"Why don't you like Adam?" she asked, not really expecting an answer. "You get along with everyone else."

At the sound of her voice, Punkin looked up, his gaze penetrating. Cats were supposed to have mystical powers. Did Punkin know something about the outcome of her relationship with Adam that she didn't?

When Adam got back, he glanced around warily. "Where is he?"

Diane's grin was slightly conspiratorial. "In the laundry room. I put his supper in there with him. Sometimes he likes to sleep on top of the dryer."

But as they settled onto Diane's couch to watch the movie, Adam forgot about the cat. Neither of them felt like popcorn, and Diane cuddled close when Adam stretched his arm across her shoulders.

While the opening credits rolled past, he smoothed back her hair and nuzzled her cheek. By the time the theme music was replaced by the opening dialogue, he had lost all interest in the screen.

She turned to look up at him and their gazes locked. When he leaned forward, she met him halfway. Kissing her was much more tantalizing than anything on the screen.

Diane's hand sifted through the hair at the back of Adam's neck, her perfume filling his nostrils and making his head swim, when an angry yowl and the sound of thumping cut across the voices on the television.

Adam raised his head and looked around, puzzled. "What's that?" He started to stand up.

"Never mind," Diane said, pulling on his hand. "It's Punkin."

The thumping sounded again, louder.

"What's he doing?" Adam asked. "Knocking on the door?"

Diane chuckled, shaking her head. "He's figured out that he can open my bedroom door if it isn't latched tight, so he thinks the same technique should work all the time. He reaches under the door with his paw and tries to jiggle it open." The banging stopped for a moment, then began again.

"He'll get tired in a few minutes and give up," she said, sliding her hands around his neck. "Now, where were we?"

Adam studied her face for a moment, then he brushed the backs of his knuckles down her cheek. "I'll show you," he murmured, covering her mouth with his.

Diane returned the kiss with a passion that left him breathless. His hands were shaking when he cupped them around her jaw and tipped it up gently, touching her mouth reverently with his own.

His face was taut with desire, and the expression in his eyes made Diane's few remaining doubts go up in smoke. A moan of need was torn from her throat as she returned his riveting gaze. She never noticed just when the noise from the laundry room stopped....

ADAM SAT IN HIS OFFICE, looking through his mail without really seeing it. He slit an envelope, glanced at the contents blindly, then tossed the whole thing onto his desk. He unfolded a brochure, held it up and then let it drop into the wastebasket without really knowing what it was. Ever since he had gotten the call that morning from L.A., he had been unable to concentrate.

Mel Forbes, highest paid game-show host in the business, was on his way to Silver Creek. He was bringing with him something that Adam had wanted to work on for a long time—a 1935 Dodge pickup truck.

He tossed the mail onto his desk. Might as well go through it some other time. He had made Mel an offer to buy the truck outright, but the other man didn't want to sell. If Adam couldn't own that truck himself, at least he had the chance to make it into something truly spectacular. When Mel arrived they were going to discuss the various ways to paint it. Adam had been thinking about it long enough that he had several ideas he thought Mel might like.

Impatiently he walked to the window again and peered out. He hadn't been this excited about a project for a long time. When would they get here?

"I'm leaving now."

Adam turned to glance at Johnny, his part-time helper. At seventeen the boy was almost as tall as Adam, and very thin. He carried his overalls folded under one arm.

"If you don't need anything else, that is." Johnny's voice, which had started to change just weeks before, cracked awkwardly on the last two words, sending color up his lean face.

Adam knew from experience that the best thing to do for the boy was to ignore the whole thing. "You sure you don't want to meet Mel?"

Johnny shook his head. "I don't watch much television."

"Okay. Go on, and have a good time."

Johnny had asked to take the rest of the day off to go waterskiing with friends. "Thanks. See you tomorrow." With a bang of the front door he was gone, riding his scooter down the road and out of sight.

Adam had called Diane's Flowers right after talking to Mel, but she was making deliveries. Maybe she would call back before Mel arrived. While he waited, Adam rechecked the bay where he would be working on the pickup. It was spotless, as was the actual paint booth. There was nothing left for him to do.

He heard someone arrive out front, and went again to the window. Diane's pink van had just pulled in, and she was walking toward the shop. Adam's eyes narrowed as he watched her slim body in her habitual shorts and shirt. Her skin looked as soft and creamy as a gardenia petal, and a predictable reaction stirred in him as he pulled the door open. He remembered the other night, when they had missed most of the James Bond movie on Diane's television. It had been worth it, too.

Now she came into his arms as if she belonged there, snuggling close. "Mmm," she said after they had shared a prolonged kiss. "What a terrific greeting."

"I'll say." Adam was tempted to kiss her again. Then he remembered the truck. "Have I got news," he said, stepping back. "I'm glad you came by."

Diane's grin widened. "I have news, too." She reached into her pocket and waved two small green rectangles of cardboard under his nose. "I got the concert tickets! A customer of mine stood in line all night, and she bought these with hers. Great seats." She was almost bubbling with excitement.

Adam had completely forgotten their conversation about the rock superstar they both liked. "Good," he said, injecting his voice with enthusiasm. "I'm glad you got them."

"I heard on the radio that they're sold out already," Diane said, tucking them carefully back into her pocket. "We were lucky."

Adam nodded, waiting impatiently to share his news. After a moment, Diane's brows rose expectantly.

"What did you have to tell me?" she asked. "You were sure looking pleased with yourself when I got here." She studied Adam's face carefully, wondering what could have excited him so much. He was usually pretty calm.

"I'm happy that you're here," he teased. "Isn't that enough reason?"

"Maybe," Diane said thoughtfully, "but I have the distinct impression that it's more than just my glowing presence."

"Well, perhaps," Adam drawled, squeezing her arm absently. "Ever since I started doing cars, there's been one old model of pickup I've wanted to work on, a '35 Dodge. The truck's a real classic. It's difficult to find one in decent shape that doesn't cost the earth and that someone is willing to sell." His eyes were dark with excitement.

"And you found one?" Diane asked, pleased for him.

Adam hesitated. "Not exactly, but the next best thing. Someone else found it, but they're bringing it here for me to work on. Mel Forbes—"

"Mel Forbes from the 'Anything Goes' game show?" Diane interrupted. She wasn't normally a game-show fan, but she did watch that one whenever she had the chance, which wasn't often.

"Yeah. He found this Dodge, and he should be here pretty soon. He wants me to look at it and probably do the body work."

Diane could hardly believe it. "Mel Forbes is coming here? To Silver Creek?" He was the hottest thing in daytime television. His show had gotten so popular that an evening version was premiering soon. And he was devastating, with thick blond hair, deep-set blue eyes and a voice that flowed like rich, dark molasses. Just the thought of seeing him in person made Diane shiver with anticipation.

"Yeah," Adam said with a frown. "He's bringing the truck up today, and we're going to figure out just how he wants it done. He plans to feature it on the debut of his evening show."

"Mel Forbes right here in Silver Creek," Diane muttered again, shaking her head. He was handsome and charming, and famous. Her hand went to her hair, which she had pulled back into a ponytail that morning. "I have to comb this out," she muttered. "And put on some lip gloss. What time is he coming?"

Adam frowned. "He's just a guy, Diane. There's no need to get all worked up." He sounded almost jealous.

"I know," she said, trying to speak calmly. "But it's not every day you get to meet a celebrity. Aren't you excited?"

Adam looked at her as if she had suddenly begun speaking in a foreign language. "I knew him in L.A., when he was waiting tables," he retorted.

"You already *know* him?" Diane almost shrieked. "Who else do you know?"

Adam shook his head, rolling his eyes. "Remember the truck," he reminded her. "The truck is what's important."

Diane realized how silly she must sound and quickly regained her composure. Adam must be disappointed in her reaction. "Well of course I can't wait to see it, either," she said, pulling the elastic band from her hair and combing through it with her fingers. "What does the truck look like?"

She was rewarded by one of Adam's sexy smiles, as he began to describe its lines, gesturing in the air with his hands. While he was talking, a cream Mercedes pulled in next to Diane's van, followed by a flatbed truck carrying something big wrapped in a huge blue tarp.

"Mel!" Adam shouted as a deeply tanned blond man got out of the car. He wore sunglasses and designer jeans.

Diane smoothed down her cotton shorts and licked her lips, then followed Adam. Mel Forbes began telling him about the trip up from L.A. as the two men turned toward the big truck. Then Adam glanced over his shoulder, following Mel's interested gaze as if he had just remembered Diane's presence. He reached out a hand and pulled her closer.

"Hi, gorgeous," Mel said after Adam had performed the introductions. Diane wished she could see beyond the tinted lenses that hid Mel's eyes. She took his outstretched hand.

"Nice to meet you."

In person, Mel was a couple of inches shorter than Adam. Even though he had the kind of looks that the camera loved, Diane could tell easily that, side by side, it was Adam who quickened her pulse rate. His dark hair was falling across his forehead and there was a smudge of grease on one cheek. His baggy overalls hid his muscular physique, making him appear bulkier than he really was, especially next to Mel who was thinner than she would have expected.

Despite all that, when Adam smiled at Diane she caught her breath. It was more than the combination of dark hair, straight nose and strong chin that attracted her. There was character in the lines that flared out from his eyes and bracketed his mouth. Intelligence glowed in his expression, and there was a primitive appeal in the way he moved that was impossible to describe but easy to see.

Adam was already pulling the tarp from the vehicle on the trailer. As chipped paint and rust spots were revealed, Diane tried hard to look impressed. The pickup could have been sitting in some farmer's field for about a hundred years. Neither Adam nor Mel seemed to notice its poor condition.

The truck driver lowered a ramp at the back of the flatbed and they began to unload the cargo as Diane called to Adam. He turned to her impatiently, obviously eager to get the new project into the shop.

"I have to go," she said quietly. "I'll try to stop back later." She waved at Mel and headed toward the van.

"She makes deliveries?" Mel asked, watching her.

"Owns the business," Adam corrected.

"Cute girl."

Adam didn't say anything and, after a moment, Mel's attention shifted back to what they were doing. "Let's get this baby unloaded," he said to the driver. "She's going to need a lot of work."

DIANE FINISHED her rounds and checked in at her shop. Things were slow and Marilyn was working all day, so Diane drove back to Adam's on her lunch hour. The other car and truck were gone, but Adam was inside, examining the old Dodge carefully as he muttered to himself and made notes on a yellow legal pad.

"Hi," he said absently, returning his attention almost immediately to the rusting truck.

"Hi, yourself," Diane responded, watching indulgently as he began to run his fingers lightly over a front fender. She had never seen him so caught up in anything before. Still, she couldn't resist going over to place a kiss on the side of his neck as he leaned down to look closely at the running board. His skin smelled of soap and after-shave and Adam.

At the touch of her lips, he straightened, his attention shifting to her. "I'm glad to see you," he murmured, bending to kiss her. Diane's hands gripped his shoulders hard as his tongue slipped inside her mouth, finding hers and stroking it. Warmth began curling through her, deep within her body as Adam continued to kiss her intimately, one hard arm anchoring her tight against him. She arched closer, moaning softly.

When he let her go, they were both breathing hard. His eyes gleamed as his attention dropped to her mouth, then back to her eyes. "On your lunch hour?" he asked.

Diane nodded. "Do you have time to stop?"

"I always have time for you." He ducked his head to kiss her again, mouth lingering against hers.

Diane's pulse had kicked into overdrive by the time he broke the kiss. She turned away, glancing around the large room. "Where's Johnny?"

Adam looked at his watch. "Gone for the day. Are you hungry?"

Something in his expression sent a fresh wave of heat through Diane. "I'm not sure how to answer that," she said candidly.

Adam chuckled, pulling her even closer. "I wondered if you had a sack lunch tucked away that you're dying to get to."

"I left it on the front seat, but I'm not starving. Why?"

He pulled her along with him to the other side of the garage. A gleaming van, taller and longer than hers, was parked there, covered with metallic paint in an ornate design.

"This is finished," Adam said. "I wanted to show you the custom interior the owner had done before he brought it in."

"Sure." The outside was too fancy for her taste, a scrollwork of flowers, birds and vines, but she gasped as he slid the side door open to reveal its interior. Almost the whole area behind the front seats was filled by a bed covered in deep green velvet. The floor was done in rich plush carpeting and the walls were paneled in oak.

"It's beautiful." She stroked the carpet with the back of her hand.

"Get in." Adam cupped her elbow, urging her inside.

Diane glanced at him and shrugged. *Why not?*

He followed her in as she sat down on the green velvet, which undulated beneath her weight.

"It's a water bed!" she exclaimed, half rising.

To her surprise, Adam shut the door behind him, closing them in the sensual cocoon, silent except for the sounds of their breathing. The only light was from two high porthole windows.

He reached over and pushed a couple of buttons on the impressive stereo that was mounted below a small bar sink on the other side. Soft music drifted from speakers in each corner of the ceiling.

A delicious feeling of languor stole over Diane as she gazed up at him in the dimness.

"Do you like it?" Adam's face was shadowed.

"I'm not sure. It's awfully decadent, don't you think?"

He chuckled as he sat next to her on the bed and trailed his fingers down her cheek. "Decadent," he echoed. "Yes, it certainly brings decadent thoughts to my head." His thumb brushed across her lower lip. "Or perhaps it's you who raised those thoughts in the first place, and this space is only encouraging them." His voice had dropped to no more than a whisper as he leaned closer and Diane shifted to meet him halfway.

"We've got our whole lunch hour," he murmured, right before his mouth covered hers.

As always, Diane melted when he kissed her. When his tongue teased her lips, she parted them on a moan. His fingers curled around her jaw, holding her head still as he adjusted the angle of his mouth to hers, exploring the dark recesses with lazy strokes of his tongue, tangling it with hers as she savored his textures. When his hands skimmed down her arms and around to her back, urging her closer still, she complied.

Diane was faintly aware of her own hands slipping across his shoulders to bury themselves in the silky hair at his nape, as her breasts settled against the hard wall of his chest.

Tendrils of smoky desire surrounded her as Adam's mouth continued to worship hers with slow, lazy strokes. Her nipples hardened as she brushed them teasingly back and forth against his chest, feeling a tremor work its way through him.

Around them the tempo of the music increased gradually, building with infinite patience to its inevitable crescendo.

Adam groaned, lifting his mouth from hers. In the gloom his face was taut with desire, cheeks hollowed, eyes blazing. One hand went to the buttons of her blouse and he began to release them, his gaze never leaving hers.

"What are you doing?" she whispered, then frowned at the foolish question.

"Doing?" Adam echoed, his voice thick. "I'm testing the van for decadence. The customer definitely wanted a decadent van."

Their mouths fused as their lips tasted and teased, passion roaring through them like a prairie fire. Then Adam groaned low in his chest, and pulled away.

His shaking fingers released the last button on her blouse. As he did so, the song ended, to be replaced by a piece full of strings and the wail of lonesome horns. It was punctuated by the occasional muted sound of traffic beyond the doors of the garage.

Within their small oasis Adam bent his head and placed a kiss on the swell of her breast above her bra. Diane raised her hands to the front of his shirt to kiss one small male nipple. Adam gasped as his fingers tangled in her hair.

She smoothed the flats of her hands across the expanse of his chest, soft dark hairs tickling her palms. Adam's head fell back as she stroked lazily downward. He was hot beneath her hands, his skin smooth, his muscles hard. Diane could feel his nerves dance as she hesitated at the waist of his jeans.

His lips skimmed across the skin of her shoulders, then he dealt with her bra, replacing the lace cups with his hands. The precious weight of Diane's breasts burned against Adam's palms. He lifted them gently toward his mouth, bending again to touch his lips to one hardened tip.

Diane moaned and arched her neck as sensation claimed her with the force of a riptide. After a moment he curled an arm around her shoulders and pulled her with him down to the undulating mattress.

"You have beautiful breasts," he said. His body's response to her touch was intense, urgent, yet he willed himself to go slowly, gripping his control with a strength he hadn't known he possessed. Again he drew a nipple into his mouth, sucking hard. "I love how you respond to me."

Diane struggled with the needs racing through her, as Adam rubbed against her intimately, arousing shattering sensations of heat and hunger. Then he stripped off the remainder of her clothes. Her body trembled with response as his fingers buried themselves in her damp curls. She gave a tiny cry, then pressed her hand to the front of his jeans. Adam's breath caught in his throat, as hot and dry as a desert wind.

Diane fumbled with his zipper, finally parting it and moving her hand inside. Adam groaned, surging against her as she gently caressed the velvety skin. When he was totally bare, she slid back up his body, covering it with her own as his arms went around her.

With a powerful movement he shifted so they were side by side. "Touch me again," he implored.

Drifting down his belly, her hand savored the texture of his skin and the contrasting feel of his dark hair, soft and then coarser. Her knuckles nudged damp, hot flesh, swollen tight against his body and before she could glide upward to capture him, Adam imprisoned her hand in his. Then he sighed and allowed it to close around him, his eyes squeezed shut as a powerful tremor shook him. Diane's fingers stroked him until he snatched her hand away.

She rose over him, burying her hot face into his shoulder as he fought to slow his breathing. After a timeless moment, she lifted his head. His eyes blazed into hers, his face dark with the desire she had raised in him. "Take me inside you."

The passion in his voice thrilled her, and the raw hunger captured her heart. "Yes," she gasped, wanting him more than she had ever wanted anything.

He grasped her hips as she settled intimately against him. Then, with a strong thrust he filled her, shuddering as he paused, buried deep, waiting for her to adjust to his possession.

"That's right, sweetheart," he rasped, as she began to move, "*so* right . . ."

"Yes," she repeated urgently as he matched her movements, "oh, yes, Adam."

He rose to meet each stroke. The breath hissed from his clenched teeth. One big hand slid around her, holding her hips tight against him as they moved faster, harder, pushing each other relentlessly over the top. Nothing existed for Diane except Adam and the things he was making her feel. She hung on tight, riding him. As passion overcame them both, he pulled her down and buried his face in her shoulder, shuddering.

Diane whirled away, as helpless as a leaf in a tornado. Only as she began to float to earth did she hear him cry out and arch against her one last time. He filled her as she held him close, tears coming to her eyes. When it was over he swept one hand down her back in long, mindless strokes. She shifted slightly and he settled her gently against him.

"Are you okay?" The sound of his voice was startling in the quiet.

"Wonderful." Her arms went around him, anchoring him close. Her heart was full of sensations, her body sated and languid.

"I wish I had the words to tell you how wonderful you make me feel," he breathed.

If Diane had had the energy to speak, she could have said the same for him. And more. Instead she touched her lips to his hot damp temple as he cradled her to him. Enjoying the warmth of his body, she drifted mindlessly.

After a few minutes he roused himself, propping his head on one elbow. Long gentle fingers smoothed her hair off her face as he smiled down at her. "You're full of secrets," he said, surprising her.

"Me? I'm transparent and uncomplicated."

Adam chuckled, shaking his head. "No way, honey. You have more layers than . . . than . . . an onion," he concluded mischievously.

Diane groaned. "How about making that a daffodil bulb, at least?"

"Okay, a daffodil," he agreed. "Every time I'm with you, I discover more. But what I'm really finding out is that the more I learn, the more I realize you keep hidden."

"I'm just a simple small-town girl," Diane told him, fingers threading through his dark hair. "What you see is what you get."

Adam sat up straighter. "Hah! You can't really expect me to believe that. You hold back a lot of yourself."

Diane raised her eyebrows. "I was with you all the way," she insisted, blushing.

Adam's arms came around her instantly. "I know that, honey. I love the way you respond to me." He hesitated, his gaze searching hers. "But I think you know that's not what I meant. What we have together is special, but you still haven't decided how far to let me into your life."

Suddenly self-conscious, Diane pulled away and reached for her clothes. Denying what he'd said would be pointless; she knew he was right and it made her uncomfortable. She turned her back as Adam sighed. She was almost done when he gently brought her around to face him. His shirt hung open over his broad chest and she had to resist the urge to caress the warm skin.

He touched her hair with his fingers. "No regrets?"

"You?" She barely breathed, waiting for his answer.

"No way. You're very special. I'm lucky to have found you." For a moment she let him hold her close, returning his light kiss. Then she stepped back, out of his arms.

He clicked off the stereo and slid the door open. Jumping down, he turned and held out a hand. His gaze was filled with something she couldn't read, mouth curved into a tender smile.

"I've kept you from your lunch," he said as she stepped down beside him. One big hand smoothed over her hair.

"And now I'm starving," Diane admitted.

"I'll get your sack and we can eat in the office." He dropped a kiss on her cheek before walking away as casually as if they'd just shared nothing more intimate than a game of cards. "Want a soda?" he asked, turning back. One hand was digging into his jeans pocket.

Diane told herself she was happy that he'd apparently decided to let things go for now. "Yes, please," she answered, feeling suddenly shy.

When Adam came into the office where she was sitting, Diane didn't meet his gaze. "Thanks," she said
when he set down her sack and the can of pop. To her
surprise, he took her hand and pulled her to her feet.

"Thank you," he said, nuzzling her neck. "For sharing something wonderful with me."

Diane hugged his waist and enjoyed the feel of him
for a moment. Then she said, "We'd better eat. I need
to stop by my mother's today or she'll think I've been
kidnapped by bandits."

Adam glanced at the wall clock, wishing that for
once she would forget all about the time. "Sure. Been
a while since you've seen her?"

Diane's chin went up. "I've been busy."

Adam grinned. "Yeah, I know." He couldn't help
darting glances at her, wondering what she was thinking as they consumed sandwiches and apples from their
respective lunches. Her cheeks were flushed, her lips
slightly swollen, her eyes that deep, mysterious purple
he found so compelling.

She looked well-loved, he thought, bemused.

A few minutes later he took her hand and walked her
to the front of his shop. The sudden ringing of his phone
made him realize that it hadn't rung the whole time they
had been in the van. Not that he would have answered
if it had.

"Call you later," he said as he held open the door.

"Okay. Go ahead and answer the phone."

He sent her one last smile and turned back inside.

"IS ANYTHING WRONG?" Diane's mother asked when
she answered the door later that afternoon, obviously
surprised to see her eldest daughter standing on her
doorstep holding a pot of pink antheriums.

Diane flushed with the guilty knowledge that she didn't often call or come by without a specific reason. "No, nothing's wrong. Am I still welcome?"

Her mother stepped back quickly. "Of course. Come in. I'm always glad to see you."

Diane dropped a peck onto her cheek and handed her the flowers before following her into the tidy living room. "I realized it had been a while since I'd come by," she said, "and I had an hour, so here I am."

Her mother set down the bouquet, exclaiming over its beauty, and pulled Diane into her arms. "I've missed you," she said, hugging her exuberantly. "Are you still working too hard?"

"Always," Diane said as they sat down. "It's the only way to get ahead."

Immediately her mother rose again. "Can I get you something to drink? Have you eaten lunch?"

Diane shook her head. "Nothing, thanks. I did eat, and I'm fine." Her thoughts wandered to her lunch companion before she pulled them sharply back to the present. "How have you been?" She was anxious to divert her mother's attention away from herself, afraid she was giving off some telltale indication of how she had spent her lunch hour.

The trim woman beside her never made any attempt to hide the fact that she thought Diane spent too much time on work, and not enough on what her mother considered was really important, finding a suitable husband and settling down. Even though Diane's two sisters had already provided her with grandchildren, she still thought Diane's life incomplete as long as she remained single. Diane's repeated attempts to explain her objective were met with worried, or even worse, pitying expressions. Her sisters, both happily married, were no help at all.

"I'm fine," her mother replied to Diane's query. "You know that I like to keep busy. I've been working more hours at the hospital gift shop, and I've been baby-sitting a lot for Christine while she attends that book-keeping course. She wants to go back to work when the children are in school."

"I hope that she's not taking advantage of you," Diane said. "My nephews are rather energetic, to put it lightly."

"I love having them. I always have time for my family."

Diane wondered if her mother was trying to make a dig at Diane's lack of attention. "I told you before I opened the shop that I'd have to work hard to make a go of it," she said, trying not to sound defensive.

Her mother raised her hand. "I know that. I've never understood why you weren't content to find a nice job until you were ready to settle down, but I haven't complained. Let's not spoil your visit now." She shifted on the couch. "Tell me, have you had time to meet anyone interesting?"

DIANE MANAGED to leave her mother's house without admitting how involved she had become with Adam. She did use the information that she had seen him several times to dam the flood of questions that were forthcoming as soon as she admitted there was a man in her life. If she had lied about only having time for business, her mother would have probably enlisted both of Diane's sisters' help in finding her a man.

Widowhood had left her mother with too much time, despite hospital volunteer work and baby-sitting, Diane thought glumly. At least the surprise of hearing her daughter confess that she was actually dating had given Diane the chance to leave without giving too much away. All she had had to promise was to come back soon, to bring Adam for a visit and to stay in closer touch by phone. *No sweat*, she thought. *I can handle that.*

FOR THE NEXT FEW DAYS, the only opportunities Diane had to see Adam were when she went by his shop. Even the steady stream of beribboned daisies had slowed to a trickle. When she called to suggest they grab a late dinner together one evening, he muttered something about microwave dinners and delivered pizzas.

"Sorry, honey. I'd love to see you, but I plan to work all evening." As she gripped the receiver, disappointed, his voice deepened, "I hated to see the green van go the other day."

"There'll be other vans, won't there?" she asked with a shiver of reaction.

"Count on it."

"How's the truck coming?" she asked.

For the next few minutes he went on at great length, describing how he had sanded, straightened and primered each fender and panel. "Sorry," he said finally. "Guess I get carried away."

"No problem." At least he remembered what they had shared, despite his preoccupation with this latest project.

"Don't forget the concert Friday," she reminded him, sure he was looking forward to it as much as she was.

"Yeah," he said vaguely. "I wonder if I'm going to have to redo one front fender. I don't like the way it came out."

Diane could tell by his tone that she had lost him, at least temporarily. "I'll see you later." She said goodbye and hung up as a little worm of jealousy began to work its way into her pleasure at his involvement with this project. Since they had last made love, Adam seemed to have become completely absorbed with the pickup, hardly a flattering commentary on what they had shared. First she had wanted him to care more about his business and now she was annoyed that he did.

You can't have it both ways, she reminded herself grumpily as she began to restock the gift card display.

By Friday Adam hadn't called her to tell her what time he would be picking her up, so she tried to call him. Johnny answered the phone on the fifth ring and she could hear loud rock music in the background. When Diane asked for Adam he wasn't there, so Johnny asked if he could take a message.

"Just tell him to pick me up at six," she said. "That way we'll avoid the inevitable traffic jam around the stadium."

Johnny promised to pass on the message and Diane went back to her own work. Reminding herself to be understanding, she began to arrange a large spray of lilies, daisies and forsythia in a wicker basket.

By six-thirty that evening she had lost both her smile and any indulgence she had left. Adam wasn't at home, he wasn't at the shop and he definitely wasn't with her. Pacing, she glared at Punkin, who had taken up residence beneath the end table, from where he watched cautiously as she went back and forth across the living room.

"Adam," Diane exclaimed aloud. "Where are you?"

After another half hour and several more fruitless phone calls, Diane glanced worriedly at the clock, then grabbed her car keys and her purse, which contained the precious tickets. She'd tried to call Carol to see if she wanted to go to the concert but there was no answer at her house, either. Diane was tempted to stay home until she heard from Adam but knew she would go crazy waiting by the phone.

"If he calls, tell him to drop dead," she told her cat. "Unless he's been hurt." There was always that possibility, but Diane was trying hard not to dwell on it.

Knowing the way the traffic would be piled up around the coliseum, she would be lucky to find her seat before intermission. The last thing she did before leaving was to flip on her message recorder, in case he did try to get in touch.

When she got home later she glanced at it again, but the message light was stubbornly dark. What if Adam *had* been hurt?

She picked up the phone and called his apartment. To her surprise, he answered on the first ring.

"Are you okay?" she asked. "I've been frantic."

"Sure," he said in an easy voice. "Why?"

7

"*WHY?*" she echoed on a screech. "Where have you been? I called the shop, I called your apartment. You weren't anywhere."

"I had to go over to a junkyard that a buddy of mine owns, for some parts for the Dodge. After I found it, we had a couple of beers. Why?"

Diane yanked the phone away from her ear and stared at it with disbelief. "If you were wondering at all how the concert was," she said, voice pure ice, "the part I heard was excellent. Of course, I did miss the first twenty minutes, trying to park the car, I got such a late start."

There was dead silence on the other end. After a moment, she said, "Adam? Are you still there?"

She heard a muffled curse. "I'll be right over," he said, and then the phone went dead.

Diane stared at the receiver in her hand, then hung it up slowly. Now that she knew Adam was okay, her worry drained away and was replaced by fresh anger, even though she told herself she should wait and find out what had happened to him. He couldn't have forgotten after all the times she had reminded him. Why hadn't he called?

She remembered his preoccupied answers when she had mentioned the concert. When she thought about it she realized that the only times she had even seen him since he'd begun work on that blasted truck were when she had stopped by his shop. A little voice inside her head asked Diane how she liked being treated the way she had treated him on more than one occasion.

"That was different," she told Punkin, who was winding his furry body around her ankles.

"Meow?" he asked, golden eyes round and innocent.

"Trust you men to stick together," Diane grumbled, stepping over him to throw herself restlessly into a chair.

Moments later the doorbell rang but she didn't get up immediately. If that was Adam, he must have broken the speed limit, but the fact still remained that he had stood her up. And he had some tall explaining to do.

A determined pounding sounded against Diane's front door. "Let me in," Adam shouted through the solid wood. "I know you're in there and I want to talk to you."

She yanked open the door and Adam almost fell into her arms. His expression was wary and distinctly uncomfortable as he righted himself and edged past her when she gestured for him to come in.

"Well?" she demanded.

"Are you going to sic Punkin on me?" he asked in a plaintive voice.

Diane's tone was grim. "That's an idea."

Adam's eyes narrowed as he peered down at her. "How angry are you?"

"How angry do you think I should be?" Her body was rigid with tension, her arms folded in front of her chest and her head thrown back as she waited for an explanation.

"I'm really sorry," Adam said in a rush. "I didn't mean to forget the concert. I know you were excited about going...." His voice trailed off and he looked suitably repentant, even rather sheepish as he shifted from one foot to the other.

New fury pumped through Diane's body as she absorbed his words. "You forgot?" She was so angry she could hardly speak. And she had been foolish enough to have worried about him! "How, pray tell, did you manage to *forget* after all the times I reminded you?" she asked through clenched teeth.

Adam tugged on one earlobe, discomfort showing plainly on his compelling features. "Uh, I had to find a new taillight fixture to replace one on the Dodge. It was pretty badly mangled." He glanced at her and then away. "I'd called a friend earlier in the week about it, and when he called back this afternoon to tell me he had one, I just dropped everything and went on down there. I didn't give the concert a thought until you called, and I'm sorry."

"I tried to call you several times," Diane commented, turning away to study the night sky beyond her living-room window. At the edge of her vision, she saw Adam raise one hand toward her and then let it drop.

"I left so fast I forgot to put the answering machine on."

Diane tried hard to control her anger as she whirled to glare at him. "How could you? I was so worried. Then I couldn't get hold of you and didn't know what to do so I went to the concert . . . but I didn't enjoy it," she finished, grumbling.

"I'm sorry," Adam repeated.

He tried to grip her shoulders but she yanked away from him, too caught up in her mixed feelings of relief and indignation.

"*Sorry!* That's it? We were lucky to get those tickets in the first place. Everyone wanted to go. If I had known you weren't going to make it I could have sold your ticket for a fortune! I could have asked Carol to go! I could have asked *anyone* and they would have been grateful." She stopped long enough to draw in a lungful of air. "I can tell you that I don't feel very important if I was so easy to forget over a . . . a taillight!" She spit out the last words as if they were the vilest of curses. "How else could I feel?"

Adam's face had darkened as he listened to her tirade. Still, he tried one more time. "It wasn't you I forgot," he said through clenched teeth. "I think of you all the time. It was the concert I forgot."

"It was going to the concert with *me!*" Diane shot back at him.

Adam raked a hand through his hair. Then he bent down until they were almost nose to nose. "How do you think *I* felt when you canceled our dates at the last minute over some two-bit emergency at the flower shop?" he asked in a low voice.

His comeback made Diane blink in surprise. "That was different," she sputtered. "Those were special circumstances." How dare he try to make her feel guilty!

"Yeah, poor planning and lack of organization," he sneered.

Accusing Diane of being unorganized was a truly low blow to her pride. "They weren't my fault," she ground out.

"They didn't make me feel very damned *important*, though," Adam said, eyes glittering.

"That's comparing apples and oranges!"

"The only difference is that I forgot to call," Adam said, "and I said I was sorry. But work is work, right? So how do you like them apples?"

Diane thought for a moment. "You're comparing a wedding to a car part. That's ridiculous."

Adam's frown deepened. "Are you saying that my work is less important than yours?" His voice was edged with disbelief.

She stared at him, pushing back her bangs. "Of course not." She began to twist a long strand of hair. "But you should be more understanding," she burst out.

Her words were like a red flag to Adam's already ragged temper. "More understanding?" he echoed. "I put up with it, didn't I? I came back for more, and I didn't get mad, even if I did want to wring your pretty neck. How much more understanding do you expect?"

"Is that why you 'forgot' the concert?" Diane asked accusingly. From the expression on Adam's face, she knew she had gone too far.

He stepped forward and gripped her upper arms, glowering darkly. "Lady, I'm beginning to wonder if you know me at all. I don't indulge in petty revenge. I didn't forget the concert to get even."

His hands tightened on Diane's arms and a sizzle of fear went down her spine. Stubbornly she thrust out her chin. "No, you just forget things that aren't important to you, like *me!*"

"That's crazy. Now you're being childish."

"Crazy! Childish! I'm not going to listen to any more of your insults." She squirmed in his grip. "And you're hurting me!"

Adam dropped his hands. Diane turned away silently. He peered closer, but she ducked her head. Feeling like a prize jerk, he captured her chin with one finger, trying to turn her face toward him. She pulled away, but not before he saw a tear spill onto her cheek. "Diane—"

She shook her head.

A brittle silence filled the living room. For a moment Adam toyed with the idea of taking the easy way out and leaving, but he knew that he couldn't. Diane meant too much to him. Obviously they still had differences and he didn't know if they could work them out but he wanted to try. The realization surprised him. Somewhere along the line, she had slipped beneath his defenses and invaded his ability to distance himself from emotional entanglements.

He swore under his breath and moved around to where he was facing her again. Her cheeks were wet and she glared at him.

"You *are* important to me," he said in a soft voice, realizing that he meant it. "I didn't mean for you to be worried. I know it sounds dumb, but it's the truth."

Diane sniffled, wiping at her cheeks. "It's just that you—"

"Shh," he whispered, placing a finger across her lips. Before she could open her mouth again, he leaned forward and pressed his lips to hers in a gentle kiss.

When he pulled away, she asked, "What was that for?"

"That was because I'm tired of arguing." Diane watched Adam's stormy gaze shift to her mouth. She knew there were things they needed to settle, but perhaps now wasn't the time to try. Emotional reaction was still pumping through her, screaming for an outlet.

Adam drew his knuckles down her cheek. His light touch made her tremble. Her mouth was suddenly dry and she swallowed. "Do you have any better ideas?" she asked.

One side of his mouth quirked. "I think I can come up with something." He grinned and she smiled back hesitantly. Then Adam bent and scooped her high into his arms. He lowered his head with infinite care, his mouth barely brushing hers. Diane forgot to breathe. The very tip of his tongue stole out to trace the line between her lips with the gentlest of strokes. She opened her mouth to him, feeling the rapid bursts of his breath against her skin. When her tongue touched his a tremor went through him and his arms tightened around her. For a timeless moment he continued the gentle caress, as if he were trying his best to erase the earlier memory of his hands biting into her arms. Diane could feel his heart drumming against his chest. Her own echoed its rhythm.

As Adam lifted his head, his gaze sought hers. His eyes flamed. Diane speared her fingers through his hair, holding his head still. Then she lifted her mouth to his and kissed him back. The heat poured through her as their lips clung.

When the kiss ended, a groan worked its way up his throat. They exchanged a look of perfect understanding. At least on one level, Diane thought, they were communicating very well.

"This could take all night," Adam said in a husky voice. "I hope you have the energy for it."

Diane slid her hands around his neck. "I have the feeling I can manage whatever stamina it takes," she purred, sifting her fingers through the hair on his nape. "As long as you're up for it." She arched a brow.

Adam's smile was brimming with bold male arrogance. "Just point me toward the bedroom and I'll show you."

She gave him directions and he carried her down the hall, shouldering open the bedroom door and kicking it shut behind them. The only light in the room was the moon glow coming through the window. Adam stopped, arms tightening.

"I want you." His expression was unreadable in the faint light.

Diane looked into his shadowed eyes. "Yes," she said simply, holding his gaze.

Bracing himself on one knee, he lowered her slowly to the bed, his eyes locked with hers. "Honey, I don't know how I've stayed away as long as I did," he murmured, following her down. "But I plan to remedy that right now."

"Yes," she repeated, "please do."

They were side by side, facing each other. Adam pulled her near, his kiss demanding a response. Beneath his tender assault, Diane melted, pressing closer. This was much better than anger. As Adam swept her with him into their own private world of passion, Diane held nothing back. Later, when their passion was spent, she collapsed on top of his heaving chest, gasping for breath. Their skin, damp with passion, pressed hotly, their legs tangled intimately. Adam's arms were spread helplessly, Diane's hung limp.

"I can't move," he gasped. "I think you've killed me."

Diane began to chuckle weakly between breaths. "What . . . a . . . way . . . to . . . go," she panted. With the very last of her strength, she managed to shift off him and curl into his side. He tucked her close with a heavy arm, and she slept.

DIANE HAD NO IDEA how much time had passed when a sound from outside woke her. Adam had shifted so that her head was pillowed against his wide shoulder. His arm still curved about her as if to prevent her from leaving. She raised up cautiously to look at his profile in the dimness, the smooth forehead and strong nose above lips that curved with sensual promise. His lashes formed thick brushes against his high cheekbones, and the line of his jaw was bold, even stubborn.

As if he sensed her stare, his lids fluttered open and he turned his head. "Hi," he whispered. "What time is it?"

"Mmm," Diane murmured, reluctant to stir. "Time to feed my cat before he starts yowling at the door."

Adam quirked a brow. "Does he wake you every night for a midnight snack?"

"No, but you're in his bed. He could object to that."

"Oh," he nodded comprehendingly. "I suppose I should go."

"Why?"

He turned to look at her more fully. "Why?" he echoed. "I don't know. Nosy neighbors? An early morning at Diane's Flowers? A dislike of male companionship across the breakfast table?"

Diane shook her head at each of his suggestions.

A slow smile curved his lips. "No? Does that mean you'll fix me breakfast?"

She thought of the banana and cold cereal she had every morning and smiled. "Sure."

"In that case, why don't you feed your cat. And tell him he can have his bed back tomorrow." Adam turned over and burrowed into the pillows.

When Diane had put an irate Punkin in the laundry room with his dishes and a folded towel to sleep on, and tiptoed back to bed, Adam appeared to be asleep. As she slid beneath the blankets, however, he revived and proceeded to convince her that there was still quite a bit of life left in him.

FOR THE FIRST TIME since she had opened Diane's Flowers Diane was late getting to the shop the next morning. She refused to let her good mood be dampened by guilt, though, as she pulled up the blinds, turned on lights and switched off the answering machine. The phone rang right away, an order for ten table decorations for a new restaurant in town. Life was good.

When Marilyn came in an hour later, Diane was busy with the accounts, for once not even minding the routine of paperwork.

Marilyn gave her a suspicious look. "Is today your birthday?" she asked.

Diane smiled brightly and then went back to the bills. "Nope."

When Marilyn continued to stare, Diane glanced up at her again. "Something I can do for you?"

"I guess not. You just look different. You didn't get your hair cut, did you?"

Diane chuckled. "No, but I probably should."

"New shade of lipstick?"

Diane thought about the evening before, the interludes in the middle of the night and again that morning, coloring as her grin widened. "Uh-uh."

"Well," Marilyn said, frowning slightly, "if you were married, I know what I'd think, but you're not."

Diane's blush deepened and she buried her head, studying an account card with fascination.

There was silence for a moment, the Marilyn suddenly snapped her fingers. "Of course. I forgot about the concert. How was it?"

"Terrific," Diane answered truthfully.

Marilyn nodded, satisfied. "Well," she said heartily, "I think I'll find something to do in the back room."

"Okay," Diane mumbled, relieved.

While she was preparing the ten centerpieces for the French Connection, Adam was forcing himself to sort though the pile of mail that had accumulated since he'd been working on the Dodge. Every few minutes, his attention would wander away and he would find himself thinking of the night before. He was sure he had a silly grin on his face and a twinkle in his eye. Johnny, who was sweeping, kept looking at him funny.

Diane never ceased to surprise him. She had been seeking him out during the last week, showing up at the garage unexpectedly just to say hello or to check on the progress of the Dodge. He wondered if she had realized yet that she was making time for him in her life, just as he wanted.

Then he recalled their argument the night before and his grin faded. How could two people who looked at things so differently come together with such total attunement? When he held Diane in his arms, nothing else mattered. Then reality intruded and they were again at odds. Adam sighed deeply, wondering if he would ever understand her.

He was still thinking about her as he opened a long envelope and began to skim over an official-looking letter. Suddenly he bit down on a curse and began again, reading more carefully. Then, with roar of anger, he grabbed his address book and jerked the telephone receiver to his ear while he stabbed out a series of numbers, swearing steadily.

A few moments later, he slammed down the receiver and balled the letter into a wad, tossing it in the general direction of the wastebasket as he kicked the metal desk with one foot. Then, fighting to control his anger, he raised his head and glared at Johnny, who was watching him through the window with a worried expression.

"What the hell do you want?" Adam snarled.

Johnny took a step back. "What's wrong?" His eyes were big in his face, which had gone pale.

Adam took a deep breath, reaching for calm. "My lease!" he shouted. "The damned landlord has canceled my lease."

"YOU'LL HAVE TO START looking for a new location right away," Diane said early that evening as they sat next to each other on the park bench in the shade. They were eating salads from the deli and watching the ducks on the small pond created and maintained by a local service organization.

Adam stabbed at a slice of hard-boiled egg. "Yeah," he grumbled.

"I mean it, Adam. You don't have much time. That letter must have sat for a week before you opened it."

One white duck, bolder than the rest, waddled over toward the bench, eyeing Diane's dinner. He quacked to himself, watching as she opened a cellophane container with two crackers inside. She held one out patiently but he would venture no closer. Finally she tossed the cracker to him. Two more ducks rushed up while he was eating it, and she broke the other cracker in half and gave it to them. After a moment the three ducks seemed to know the free lunch was over and they went back to the pond, tail feathers wagging as they gossiped among themselves.

"I don't want a new location," Adam said. His jaw was set as he lifted his gaze and impaled her with his dark eyes. "I'm happy where I am."

"You don't have a choice. Your landlord is selling the property, you told me yourself. He won't renew your lease. They're going to build an office complex there."

"I've got a little over two weeks," he said, biting through a carrot stick with a snap of white teeth.

"The time will go fast," she cautioned.

"I'll look when I'm done with the Dodge."

"Adam!"

"HE HASN'T DONE ANYTHING about it," she complained to Carol several days later. "At this rate he'll be out on the street before he knows it."

"So do the looking for him." Carol had a practical streak.

"I don't have time."

"You can make the time," Carol insisted, "Marilyn and I will cover for you. You take my car and I'll make the deliveries."

Diane thought about it a minute. "Perhaps you're right. Someone has to save him from his own procrastination."

She picked up the phone and called Adam.

"Have you found anything yet?"

His sigh was audible over the wires. "This constitutes borderline nagging," he cautioned.

"That means no. So what exactly do you need in a building?"

He thought a moment and then reeled off a list of requirements that Diane did her best to write down. "Well," she said, "I don't want to keep you. Talk to you later." With luck, she would have a selection of locations for him to consider before his lease had expired.

Next Diane hauled the phone book out from under the counter and called the first real estate agent who handled rentals, setting up an appointment for later that day. When they met and began to search through the commercial listings, Diane was disappointed to find out that, Silver Creek being a small town, there were few options. One place that would have been ideal wouldn't be vacant for two months. Another would take extensive remodeling. A third was in an impossible location, with an impossible rent.

Finally, after the agent had gone through every possibility she had and the two of them had spent several afternoons checking out everything remotely suited to Adam's needs, they found a site Diane thought would do. It filled his basic requirements, having most recently been occupied by an automobile mechanic who had moved his business to a neighboring town. It wasn't too far from Adam's present location and was roomy enough, with a concrete floor, roll-up doors and a big parking lot. Now the challenge would be to get Adam to look at it. He was almost done with the pickup; perhaps Diane could tear him away.

She thought of how long it had been since she had spent any real time with him, and how much she missed him. "There's one problem," she told the agent, who was jotting notes onto a pad.

"What's that?"

Diane felt a twinge of guilt for deceiving her, but it only lasted a moment. "Adam's rather eccentric. You know how these artistic types can be."

The agent's eyes narrowed. "Eccentric?"

"In a very successful way," Diane hastened to relieve her. "It's just that, well, I'm afraid if we make an appointment, I might not be able to persuade him to keep it. If he's in the middle of a creative spell."

The agent looked worried. No doubt she could see her commission disappearing. "He's not unreliable, is he?"

"Oh, no. He's as reliable as tomorrow's sunrise, once he signs the papers. If I could just borrow the key—"

"Impossible."

Diane's spirits sank. She tried again. "You see, that way, if I did talk him into it, he wouldn't have all that time to change his mind while I called you and we made arrangements. I could just whisk him over there while he was in the mood."

"I just can't do it," the agent said firmly.

Diane sighed. "The property is vacant, isn't it?"

"Yes."

"And empty. Then what harm could there be? You know it's the only place in town that's really suitable. I'll show it to him and drop the key off here afterwards. Or first thing in the morning, at the latest."

The agent seemed to be weakening. "You really think it's the only way?"

"I know it is," Diane said.

The agent drummed her acrylic nails on the top of her desk. "You won't tell anyone?"

Diane smiled. "Cross my heart."

"Okay. I'll bring the key by your flower shop," she said. "And you be sure to get it back to me."

"I promise." Diane smiled, her thoughts rushing ahead to how pleased Adam would be. She was certainly getting more impulsive since she'd met him.

"OH, ALL RIGHT!" Adam rolled his eyes. "I guess that if you took the time to look, I could at least see what you've found."

Diane, who had been nagging him steadily for twenty minutes, took a deep breath. "Let's go."

"Now?" Adam glanced down at his dirty coveralls and dirtier hands. "How about tomorrow?"

"No. Now."

His hopeful smile faded and he began to strip off his coveralls, revealing reasonably clean jeans and a yellow T-shirt. "Okay, okay. Do I have time to wash my hands?"

Diane ignored the irritation in his tone. "Sure."

A half an hour later, after Adam had thoroughly inspected the property, enthusiasm broadened his grin.

He enveloped Diane in a bear hug. "I think you've got it!" He gave her a brief, hard kiss.

"There's one drawback," she said, pulling away.

His smile faded. She had already told him about the problems with the other places she had looked at. "What?" he asked.

"The rent." She named a figure that was almost double what he was currently paying, which had been an extremely reasonable sum.

Adam frowned. "Ouch."

"Too much?"

He looked around again. "No, I guess not. Couldn't get by on my looks forever, I guess. I'll just have to put in a few more hours."

Diane batted him playfully. "Somehow I don't think that will kill you."

Her provocative grin was giving him ideas. He cleared his throat. "I really appreciate your finding this place," he said. It hit him that Diane had taken time away from work to look, putting his needs ahead of her own business.

"I'm glad you like it," she said. "There wasn't much to choose from."

"I can imagine." The more he thought about what she had done, the more pleased he became.

They stood smiling at each other, Diane's eyes glowing and her cheeks rosy with pleasure. Adam's gratitude was beginning to get tangled with the other feelings just looking at her were arousing in him. He crossed to the door and locked it, hooked an arm around her waist and drew in her scent of wildflowers and woman.

"Let's check the office out again."

Cuddling close to his lean frame, Diane went with him. The room was a small one, with no windows. Several quilted pads were folded and piled in one corner.

"Someone left these when they moved," he said, spreading a couple of them on the cement floor.

Diane watched him curiously. Instead of switching on the light, he had left the door open enough so that some illumination from the main room filtered inside.

"What are you doing?"

He tested the pads' softness, then straightened, slipping his arms back around her.

"Thanking you properly," he growled.

His first hungry kiss melted away her objections. The second sent her temperature soaring and urged her hands to slip beneath the hem of his T-shirt, to caress the bare, hot skin of his back, and the third made her knees give way, sinking them both into the nest of quilts.

In moments they'd stripped and come together with fiery urgency. Diane received Adam's thrusts with little cries of encouragement. When she began to quiver helplessly around him, he groaned raggedly and gripped her tightly as they exploded together with the urgency of untamed passion.

ADAM SIGNED THE LEASE with the real estate agent in the morning, wondering uncomfortably why she kept giving him strange looks when she thought he didn't notice. After the formalities were done, he made arrangements with several friends to help him move the next weekend. In the meantime, he finished the Dodge on schedule and delivered it to Mel Forbes, who was extremely pleased with the results.

The pickup's smooth, undented body was now covered with midnight-blue metallic paint, its side windows each sporting an etched rosebud in one corner. A matching rose, done in white, graced the driver's door.

"You're a genius," Mel exclaimed when Adam delivered the truck to L.A. "I'm almost grateful enough to agree to sell it to you, but not quite." He laughed and Adam forced a smile.

"If you should change your mind about that—" he began.

"I'll let you know," Mel finished for him.

"Good luck on the new show," Adam told him, pocketing the hefty check Mel had immediately written out. Before the other man could launch into one of his long monologues about the entertainment business, Adam made his excuses and left, eager to get back to Silver Creek.

He had called his father that morning but wasn't surprised that the busy surgeon didn't have time for lunch. Adam didn't mind leaving the hectic pace and the smog of L.A. far behind him, and now Diane gave him an added reason to hurry home.

He told himself that it was the memory of her sweet, responsive lovemaking that drew him, but he was having trouble accepting that explanation. He remembered the time she had taken to look for his new location. Perhaps they were both finding room for each other in their lives. Somehow the thought didn't unnerve him as much as it usually did. He could hardly imagine life without her. With a last glance behind him at the smog-shrouded city, Adam began the long drive home.

8

THE NEXT WEEK was a busy one for Diane, who put in some long hours to make up for the time she'd taken off. Marilyn had suggested she increase her standing order with the wholesaler who delivered to the shop three times a week, and Diane had to be sure she wasn't ordering too much. Wasted flowers were a drain on her profit margin. She and Marilyn spent several hours deciding what they needed, and Diane found that the older woman's extensive experience was an added blessing.

Adam had moved and was settling in at his new location, grumbling lightly about the higher rent. Perhaps now he would accept the idea that a degree of success was sometimes justified. He had thanked Diane several more times, and she discovered that she liked feeling needed, especially by Adam.

The next weekend Diane was taking him to meet her family at a birthday party her sister, Jean, was throwing for their mother. "I'd like to meet them," Adam had responded over the phone. "It's a chance to understand you better."

Perhaps that comment should have concerned her more, but she didn't have time to dwell on it.

"You'll have to promise to ignore the machinations of my two sisters," she told him. "Since they're both married with children, they think it's the only fit state for everyone."

Adam chuckled indulgently. "Matchmakers, are they?"

Diane nodded. "And not too subtle, I'm afraid. With you there, they can only be worse."

"That's okay. They haven't met *my* sister."

Diane laughed, relieved that he understood.

The day of the family barbecue dawned hot and sunny. When Adam came by to pick Diane up, she hadn't yet wrapped her mother's present. He was wearing shorts and beneath them his legs were richly tanned and roped with long muscles. The tank top he wore fit snug across his wide chest, revealing the sweep of his broad shoulders and his powerful arms. Remembering how they felt wrapped around her, Diane eyed him possessively, eager to see her sister's reactions to this gorgeous hunk who was escorting her. There was always the hope they would be too bowled over to make embarrassing remarks about her single state.

"Does your mom wear a lot of jewelry?" Adam asked, looking at the earrings and necklace Diane had bought her.

"She didn't use to," Diane replied absently, returning her attention to the flowered paper she had been about to fold around the gift box. "Now that things are easier, I like her to have a few luxuries."

Adam stepped behind her to massage her shoulders, which were surprisingly tense beneath the straps of her jumpsuit. His strong fingers urged her to relax and Diane sighed her appreciation.

"You said your father died a few years ago, didn't you?" His deep voice was gentle.

"Yes, three years ago. Heart attack. It was very sudden." She pictured her dad's lined face with its customary smile, blue eyes warm below his habitual gray crewcut. She still missed talking to him. After she had been silent for a moment, Adam touched her cheek.

"That's rough," he said as his fingers caressed her lightly.

"I still miss him." Diane swallowed past the lump in her throat before continuing. "We were all surprised to discover afterward that he had taken out a substantial life insurance policy on himself. At least Mom's had no money worries."

"A sudden death is always hard to deal with," Adam said slowly. Diane thought about what he'd said as she wrote on the birthday card. He'd lost his wife unexpectedly, so he would know all about dealing with that. "I don't imagine it's ever easy." She slid her mother's card into its envelope, wanting to ask if Adam had really accepted his wife's death, but not quite daring.

"I brought a couple of bottles of wine," he said after a moment, changing the subject. "Will that be okay?"

"What a nice idea." Diane glanced up to see that he was holding out a small package wrapped in pink and white striped paper.

"This is for you."

"Me? You didn't have to do that." She accepted the gift, flustered.

"I wanted to." He chuckled. "Actually, when I saw it, I couldn't resist."

She stared at him puzzled.

"Open it," he urged, "and you'll see what I meant."

Diane pulled off the bow and unwrapped the paper. The name of a gift shop in the new mall south of town was embossed in silver on the box. Adam hadn't just happened to have seen it there. He must have been looking. She lifted the lid and unwound the tissue paper.

"Oh!" she gasped when she had uncovered the contents. "It's adorable."

"See what I mean," he asked, sounding pleased. "How could I have resisted?"

In her hand Diane held the figurine of a plump orange cat surrounded by daisies. Her finger stroked the tiny animal's head as she admired the delicate coloring, then she cradled the figure in her hand and reached to kiss Adam on the cheek.

"Thank you," she murmured, deeply touched. "I love it."

"It's a little reward for finding more time for me," Adam said gruffly before his mouth found hers. After a moment in which Diane's pulse slammed into overdrive, he released her.

"Well," she said, trying to keep the tremor of reaction from her voice. "I suppose we'd better get going." She set the porcelain figure carefully in a place of honor on her bookcase, then finished wrapping the jewelry for her mother. Pointing at a bonsai tree in an oriental pot that she had brought home from the shop, she asked, "Would you mind carrying that?"

He lifted the plant gingerly. "Sure."

She stuffed the birthday present and card into her oversized purse, and took a covered dish from the fridge. "Potato salad," she explained when Adam glanced at it and raised an inquiring brow.

"You made it yourself?"

"With these two hands. I was up at seven, boiling potatoes and eggs."

"I'm impressed." He grinned. "All set?"

She looked around. "I think so."

"What about Punkin?"

"He and Jean's Golden Lab don't see eye to eye." She bent down to peer at her cat, who was sitting on a kitchen chair. "See you later, baby."

Punkin gave her a cold stare.

"I don't think he likes the idea of my leaving with you," Diane teased Adam. He hadn't said another word about winning the cat over since Punkin had insulted his gift of fish.

Adam snorted as they went out the front door. "Maybe *I* don't like the idea of you sleeping with *him*."

Diane followed him and saw that her nosy neighbor from the adjoining duplex was standing in her doorway. Since her mouth was hanging open, Diane assumed the woman had heard Adam's misleading remark.

"Well, I hope you don't expect me to choose between the two of you," Diane said airily. "Hello, Mrs. Burn."

Her neighbor mumbled a reply, frowning with disapproval at Adam. Then she went inside and slammed the door.

"Sorry about that," Adam drawled.

Diane smiled broadly. "Don't worry about it."

Her good mood lasted until they got to the party.

When she introduced Adam to Jean, her sister's eyes widened as she studied him with obvious approval. Then Jean turned to Diane.

"Congratulations," she said cheerfully. "I'm glad to see that you've finally gotten your priorities straight and found yourself a man with definite possibilities."

While Diane made a mental note to throttle her sister the next time she saw her, Adam chuckled and shook Jean's hand. "Thank you," he said gravely. "I see that beauty runs in the family."

While Jean held Adam's hand a moment too long, looking totally flustered, Diane recovered quickly and turned to introduce him to her mother and her other sister, Christine.

"Happy birthday, Mom," Diane said, giving her the wrapped present and the bonsai. It was always a bit of a shock to see her mother in trim slacks and coordinated top, with her now silver hair short and neatly permed, after so many years of faded house dresses and hair pulled back into a ponytail.

"Thank you, sweetheart. I'm glad you could make it today."

Her words made Diane search the lined face for any signs of reproach, but there were none. They hugged and Diane kissed her soft cheek, breathing in the lavender scent her mother had always favored.

"This is my friend, Adam," she said, stepping back.

"It's nice to meet you." Diane's mother gave him a warm smile.

"You, too, Mrs. Simmons. Happy birthday."

"Look, Adam brought some wine," Diane said before Jean could say anything else to embarrass her.

"How thoughtful." After the rest of the introductions were made, Diane's mother handed the bottles to Jean's husband, Jack. "Put these in the fridge, will you, dear?" Then she linked arms with Adam. "Tell me about yourself while the kids get the food ready."

Adam looked at Diane over her mother's shoulder, and he gave her a reassuring wink. Diane had no choice but to get her potato salad out of his car and proceed to the kitchen.

"Is it serious?" Christine asked as she arranged raw vegetables on a plastic tray.

Diane evaded her sister's curious stare, glad that Adam was too far away to overhear. Lord only knew what her mother was asking *him*. Removing the lid from the potato salad, Diane did her best to avoid giving Christine a straight answer. "What do you mean by 'serious'? We aren't engaged or anything like that."

Christine moved closer. "Are you sleeping with him?"

Diane felt her face go hot. "Chris! I didn't ask you that about Jim when you started dating, did I?"

"Only because you weren't around enough to get the chance. But I bet you wondered."

"I didn't have time to wonder," Diane said dryly. "I was too busy working two jobs. Where is Jim, anyway?"

"He went to get ice."

Before Christine could ask any more nosy questions, Diane went out the back door to join her mother and Adam. When he saw her coming, he reached out a hand. "We've been talking about the pros and cons of small-town life versus living in L.A.," he said.

"Since Adam grew up there, I thought he might miss the big city, but he assures me that he doesn't." Diane's mother smiled at the two of them, her gaze flicking to their joined hands. "He intends to stay here."

"Of course he does," Diane said, irritated that her mother found it necessary to ask about Adam's future plans. "His business is here."

Adam's grip tightened on her hand. "Among other things."

"You didn't get to meet Christine's husband," Diane said hastily. "I think I just heard his car." Sending her mother a quelling glance, she pulled him toward the house.

Later, after everyone had eaten, finishing with birthday cake and ice cream, Adam showed Jack his '55 Chev while Jim kept track of the children who were splashing in a small wading pool in the backyard. Diane helped put away the leftover food. She waited nervously for the questions to start but, to her surprise, her mother and sisters just talked about the children.

"I didn't know Jimmy had chicken pox," Diane commented after Chris had complained about how bored he'd been while he was home from nursery school.

"You would have if you'd returned my last phone call, but you were probably too busy." Christine's tone was offended.

"I'm sorry," Diane said, feeling guilty. She gave her sister's waist a squeeze. "I'll try to do better."

Chris rolled her eyes and grinned. "Don't strain anything," she teased.

Diane was pleased that she wasn't going to hold a grudge.

"If you plan to turn over a new leaf, I'm having a candle party Tuesday night," Jean began.

"Thanks anyway," Diane replied with a grin as Chris groaned. Jean was always having the kind of parties where the guests bought candles, crystal, plastic ware or any number of other items so the hostess could obtain a free gift. Over the years, Chris and Diane had learned to avoid them or end up buying something they didn't really need.

As she helped her two sisters, Diane felt closer to them than she had in a long while. Perhaps she did need to find more time for her family.

When the work was done, they all sat around on lawn chairs finishing the wine and watching the toddlers while Jack, holding the baby, played with them.

"Jack reminds me of your father," Diane's mother told her, watching him roll on a beach ball toward his son. "Joe was always there to help with you kids, bandaging scraped knees, wiping runny noses and giving hugs. I guess he was ahead of his time."

"I miss him," Jean said wistfully. "If he wasn't at work he was with us."

"That was where he wanted to be," their mother said.

Diane glanced at Adam, who was following the conversation with interest. "That dead-end job of his didn't require any overtime," she couldn't help but say. "If he had gone to night school or taken classes he could have found something better, something that paid more." And they wouldn't have been so poor, she added silently.

"He preferred to spend his spare time with his family," Diane's mother repeated quietly. "He never finished high school and he may not have had some fancy job or paperwork to bring home every night, but he was always there to listen, to repair things around the house, to help me when I needed him. He never missed a school play or band concert when one of you was in it."

For a moment everyone was silent, thinking their own thoughts. Then an argument broke out between two of the children who each wanted to play with the same toy. Jean and Chris both got up to referee.

"Adam and I had better be going," Diane told her mother. "We both have to work tomorrow." Her words preceded the beginnings of a general exodus.

As everyone began gathering up kids, food and other possessions, Diane's mother gave Adam a warm hug.

"Thanks for coming," she said, "and for bringing the wine. Everyone enjoyed it."

She was wearing the jewelry Diane had given her. "Don't be such a stranger, and bring Adam back, too," she told Diane before turning to speak to Jean.

"WELL, WHAT DID YOU think?" Diane asked him as they drove away from Jean's ranch house.

"Nice family," Adam said, his face shadowed in the evening darkness. "Your father sounds like he was quite a man."

"What do you mean?" Diane's voice was sharper than she had intended.

Adam remembered his own childhood and the busy doctor—his father—who was hardly ever home and was often called away on birthdays and family holidays. Somehow the wealth of presents had never made up for his absence. "He must have spent a lot of time with you."

"I guess he did," Diane admitted rather grudgingly, "but I used to wish he'd do something to better himself and our own lot. He'd come to open house or teacher's conferences at school in his janitor's uniform. It seemed like the other dads always wore suits and worked in offices."

"At least he came." Adam couldn't remember his father ever going to a school function, including the father-son football field trip or the play Adam had been in during his junior year. And he had only managed to see one of the basketball games Adam played. One in four years.

Adam reminded himself that it no longer mattered. "'Money isn't everything,'" he quoted.

"Hah. Spoken like a person who's never lacked for it." Diane's tone was bitter.

"Were you really poor?" he asked gently.

"Sometimes," Diane said. "We had no medical benefits and the plant where Dad worked didn't believe in paid holidays or vacation for the janitorial staff. When things got real slow, they didn't work. One winter Dad was really sick and we didn't have much of a Christmas."

Diane was silent for a moment. "That sounds selfish," she said. "No matter how bad it got, we had each other. Eventually when we got older we got jobs. One summer we picked fruit, but I couldn't climb the ladders because of my fear of heights. I used to envy other kids, other families."

"I can understand that it was difficult," Adam said as he glanced at her, noticing how pretty she was in the growing dusk, "but some of those kids might have envied you." In a lot of ways, he did.

He remembered Penny's hunger for the finer things. She had grown up in a large middle-class family, and had always longed for the trappings of success, especially after she started running with minor-league celebrities. Was Diane the same way, putting possessions ahead of people, and success ahead of relationships? He thought about the simple life she led, and how hard she worked. He remembered their lovemaking. No, Diane wasn't like that, he was sure of it.

Beside him, Diane was thinking about the time her father had been very sick and had stayed home from work for three weeks. When she got home from school each day, she would go into her parents' bedroom, taking him a glass of apple juice and sprawling across the foot of the bed while she told him about her day. He was always interested, no matter how tired he seemed. Her mother was worried that Diane would catch the flu but she never had, and she had actually been disappointed when he went back to work. She'd forgotten all about that time.

"My father was hardly ever home for Christmas," Adam said. "He was usually on call at the hospital. When I got older, Mom would take Lori and me skiing over the holidays and one winter the three of us went to Mexico for a week."

"And your father didn't go?"

"Never. Something would always come up. Dad was, and is, a dedicated workaholic."

The image of a small, dark-haired boy with sad brown eyes waiting for his father to come home for Christmas plucked at Diane's heartstrings until she remembered that Adam had been skiing or on the beach in Mexico during this parental neglect. Her sympathy faded.

"You didn't have it so rough," she said.

Adam's mouth thinned. "You don't know. Your father was always there."

For a moment she returned his glare, then she looked out the window, suppressing an angry retort. What did he know?

Adam, too, was thinking about what she had told him. He could see how her father's apparent lack of ambition had shaped her own drive to succeed. Just as he had been influenced by his childhood, so had she.

Adam saw Diane's big orange cat sitting in the front window when he pulled into the driveway to her duplex. "I don't think I'll come in," he said, glancing at his watch. "You probably have things to do."

Diane's feelings were mixed. She was annoyed he didn't understand the way she felt about her childhood, but she didn't want him to leave while things weren't quite right between them. She didn't want him to think less of her; he mattered too much for that. While she was trying to deal with her feelings, he turned to pull her against him and kissed her.

"Thanks for taking me with you. I enjoyed meeting your family." For a moment he looked as if he was going to say more, then he must have thought better of it. Instead he pushed aside her bangs with one finger and kissed her forehead. "I'll walk you up," he said, getting out to open her door.

"Thanks again for my present," Diane said.

Later that night when she was in bed, she tossed and turned as she tried to put things into the familiar perspective of work first, but her feelings toward Adam refused to remain on the fringes of her life. She lay awake for a long time, staring into the darkness and wondering about the future.

WHILE ADAM WAITED to start the next big project, he busied himself with small jobs, replacing a crumpled fender, changing the color of a teenager's VW Bug from white to fire-engine red. It was the kind of routine work he often hadn't bothered with in the past, but now he had serious rent to pay. Still, he always knew that if he were absolutely desperate and had nowhere else to turn, his father would help if Adam asked. How carefree would he be if, like Diane, he had no one to rely on but himself? It was a question he couldn't answer. And it wasn't enough to stop him from wanting her company when he did have time off.

"You told me that Marilyn can handle anything," he said to her over lunch. They were seated in the side yard of a popular submarine sandwich shop, surrounded by hanging baskets filled with colorful fuchsias and flower boxes bursting with red and pink petunias. The place was packed. Diane was wearing the daisy he'd brought with him behind one ear.

"Carol's coming in, too," he added. "Take the afternoon off. Like you said before, nothing went wrong while you were out looking at rental property. What fun is being the boss if you can't do what you want at least some of the time?"

The smile tugging at the corners of Diane's full mouth gave him hope that she was weakening. A tiny frown appeared between her elegantly arched brows as her violet eyes met his and then danced away, resting on his fingers that were drumming an impatient tattoo on the tabletop.

Adam moved closer, curving an arm around her shoulders, his fingers toying with the lace trim of her short-sleeved light blue blouse. Its stand-up collar, trimmed with more lace, framed her face. "You've been working hard to catch up all week. You need a break."

"You think so?" she asked.

"I know so. Trust me."

Across from him Diane sighed. "I'm not sure that's such a good idea. You could be a bad influence on me."

A devilish grin slashed across Adam's face as he slapped one hand over his heart, covered by his blue chambray work shirt. "Would I do that?"

Diane wisely refused to answer, but over the next couple of weeks she did seem to be making an effort to learn how to relax and to spend more time with him. They put the top down on the Chevy and drove though the country around Silver Creek, lingering over quiet picnics by the river. Adam borrowed a bicycle for her and they went on long rides together, talking about inconsequential things as they pedaled down quiet side roads, stopping to exchange kisses when no one else was around.

Adam taught her to fish along Silver Creek, and she caught three small trout that she proudly showed off to Punkin after the two of them had ridden back to her apartment to cook them for supper that evening. Punkin sniffed at the fish curiously and even deigned to share their feast, nibbling the morsels that Diane gave him. They went to a barbecue at Adam's sister's house, and Diane was pleased to see that she and Tom still had the happy glow they'd worn at their wedding.

Best of all, Diane and Adam made love—tender, leisurely, passionate love. Indoors, outdoors, in the dark of night and the heat of the afternoon.

"You know," she said one day as she walked the bikes back to Adam's apartment, "after I've been away from the shop, I'm more excited to get back there, as if I've been recharged."

"That's the whole idea," Adam told her, unlocking his door. "What do you think weekends were invented for?"

They went inside to change into swimsuits so they could cool off in the pool, but somewhere between the front door and the bedroom, Adam was distracted by the sight of Diane's slim legs and the image of how good they felt wrapped around him. A short while later, as he held her in his arms, snuggled against his heart, it occurred to him that he hadn't changed Diane. She was doing that herself.

Perhaps, with her at his side, he could finally lay down the guilt he felt over Penny's death. Maybe he truly hadn't been responsible for her problems, and maybe the only person you *could* change was yourself.

CAROL HAD A dentist appointment one morning, Marilyn was making deliveries and the shop was surprisingly busy, the phone and walk-in business keeping Diane hopping.

"Diane's Flowers," she recited automatically, as she picked up the receiver on the second ring. "How may I help you?"

The confident voice on the other end introduced herself as Georgia Morgan, assistant to the president of the bank that was opening across from the new shopping mall at the edge of town. Quickly she outlined their needs for the grand-opening celebration, including corsages for the female employees and boutonnieres for the men. While she was speaking, Diane did some quick figuring on a scratch pad of paper.

"Of course we can accommodate you," she said more confidently than she felt. The bank also wanted several hundred carnation boutonnieres to give away to everyone who came in during the grand opening, an extremely large order for Diane's small staff to handle, but with the proper planning and preparation she was sure they could pull it off.

"Let me do some figuring and I'll call you back with a price," Diane told her.

Ms. Morgan assured her she would be waiting to hear. Diane knew that while she was eagerly waiting, she would also be calling every other florist in town for quotes. Diane consulted a cost sheet, did some multiplying on her calculator, double-checked her figures, called her wholesaler and then thought a moment about whether she had overlooked anything. Satisfied that she had the best price possible, she called Ms. Morgan back.

She promised to give Diane an answer later in the week.

"Don't wait too long," Diane cautioned her. "I'll need to special order that large a quantity from my supplier, and we'll be cutting it close as is."

After she said goodbye and hung up, Diane began to wonder if she should have turned down the opportunity. As long as she got the flowers in time and nothing unexpected happened, and if things went exactly as planned they would be able to carry it off. And the publicity would be great for business. It was worth the gamble, she decided resolutely.

The next day, Georgia Morgan came by to introduce herself and accept Diane's bid. They made final arrangements and filled out the paperwork. Since it was such a large order, Ms. Morgan gave Diane a substantial deposit. After the woman left, Diane and Marilyn gaped at the check for a while before Diane stamped the back and put it into the bottom of the cash drawer.

"I think we've hit the big time," Marilyn said.

"Now all we have to do is to pull it off." Diane's voice was dry as she did her best to hide the doubts that insisted on plaguing her. She picked up the phone to call Adam, but halfway through dialing she wondered if he would approve of her accepting such a large order, one that would take a lot of her time and strain her resources. Frowning, she hung up. Over the next few days, she was tempted to tell him what she had done, but something always stopped her.

The morning the bank's flowers were due to arrive, Diane was gingerly trying to move a display plant with one hand and persistent nudges of her hip when Marilyn came in the front door.

"Today's the day," she said cheerily. "I hope you're ready to wrap carnations."

Diane said nothing, silently holding up one arm.

Marilyn's mouth dropped open. "What did you do to yourself?" she demanded, staring.

Diane glanced ruefully at the thick Ace bandage. "Sprained my wrist," she said, holding it up for Marilyn to see.

Marilyn clucked sympathetically. "How did you manage to do that?"

Diane's grin was sheepish. "Don't laugh," she cautioned. "I feel clumsy enough. Would you believe I tripped over my cat? I was running for the phone and he decided, with perfect timing, to dart across the kitchen. When I started to fall I caught myself against the counter, almost bent my wrist double, and the rest is history."

"Who was on the phone?" Marilyn asked.

"Someone trying to sell aluminum siding, and I live in a rental."

"I wouldn't laugh at you," Marilyn said, "only because my husband broke his foot when he got up to change the channel on the television and tripped over our bulldog who always sleeps in front of him."

"Did he shoot the dog?" Diane couldn't help but ask. For a moment the evening before she had been tempted to shoot Punkin, who had fled to the safety of the bedroom closet.

"No, but we got a remote control the next week. And I sympathize with your injury."

"My timing isn't the best," Diane said ruefully.

"How long do you have to take it easy?" Marilyn asked, obviously noticing it was Diane's right wrist that had been injured.

"A couple of weeks."

"It's a good thing we have two days to do the carnations for the bank. It doesn't look like you'll be much help."

"I know," Diane agreed. She'd thought of nothing else the whole time she'd been waiting in the emergency room the night before. She had thought of calling Adam at the time, but then decided not to bother him.

"Why didn't you tell me?" he asked when he stopped by an hour later. "I would have been glad to drive you to the hospital and to hold your good hand while you waited." His eyes were dark with concern.

Diane shrugged. "It always takes forever at the emergency room," she said. "I didn't want to keep you there all night."

He bent closer, his steady gaze compelling. "Where would I rather be at night than with you?" he whispered. "One of these days we'll have to discuss that."

Diane stared, not sure what to say. Lucky for her, the ringing telephone saved her from having to answer.

"Excuse me." She slipped by him and captured the receiver.

"About your special order," the wholesaler said without preamble. "I can't send the flowers until tomorrow afternoon. One of my trucks is in the shop today, and the other one's going in the opposite direction from you."

"No!" Diane felt the blood drain from her head. Her worst nightmares were coming true! She turned her back on Adam, who was watching her curiously. "I have to have them today or we'll never get the boutonnieres done in time. I promised them to the bank first thing Wednesday morning."

The supplier apologized profusely but there was nothing he could do to speed things up, though he did assure her that the truck would definitely be there the next day.

"I understand," Diane said, glumly. "It isn't your fault that I took such a large job."

"I'm sorry," he said, sounding genuinely regretful. "Good luck with your boutonnieres."

Diane thanked him and hung up, resisting the urge to slam the receiver down out of pure frustration. Her shoulders slumped as she tried to think what to do.

Adam slid his arm around her. "Trouble?"

"I can't believe this is happening," Diane wailed, too upset to keep the news from him any longer as she was suddenly overcome with the gravity of her predicament. In clipped sentences she explained the problem.

"I'll go get them right now," Adam offered.

"No." Diane put a detaining hand on his arm. "Thank you, but that won't work. They're delivered in a refrigerated truck and today's heat must be a record."

"There's gotta be something I can do." Adam began to pace, his dark brows furrowed with concentration. "How complicated is making the boutonnieres?" he asked.

"Not complicated at all. A child could do it. Why?" Diane was fidgeting with a lock of her hair, wishing she had never heard of the huge order or the new bank.

"Call your family," he suggested. "Aren't they all free in the evenings? I'm sure that Tom and Lori will be glad to help, too. And of course I'll come." He glanced down at her bandaged wrist. "You can supervise. We'll have a work party tomorrow night and be done in no time."

Diane's eyes widened at his suggestion and she thought for a moment. They just might pull it off. If they didn't, her reputation as a reliable businessperson would be completely ruined.

"You're a genius," she exclaimed, hugging him.

Before his arms could close around her waist, she stepped back. "No time," she said, grinning. "I have to make some phone calls."

She called her mother and explained the situation. Ten minutes later, her mother called back. "It's all set. Jack will watch all the children. Jim, Jean, Christine and I will be at your shop at about six o'clock tomorrow night, as soon as Jim gets off work. We'll stay until the job's done."

"Oh, Mom, I really appreciate this!"

"I guess it's to be expected when you have a workaholic for a daughter," her mother teased before she said goodbye. "See you tomorrow."

There was that word again. Workaholic. Adam had described his father that way. No wonder he had trouble with Diane's dedication to business.

She threw herself into his arms. "It's going to be okay," she said. "I can feel it." This time, when his arms closed around her, she burrowed into his shoulder, savoring the feeling of comfort and protection his embrace provided. A wave of love washed over her, making her stiffen within the circle of his arms. Resolutely she pushed the feeling aside. *I have no time for this*, she told herself. *I'll deal with it later.*

Adam, having no idea what was going through her head, lifted her and swung her around before he released her.

"You're right," he said. "I think it's going to work."

Diane could only wonder if they were talking about the same thing.

THE NEXT DAY, the delivery truck finally showed up in the late afternoon. Diane and Marilyn had gotten the rest of the supplies ready, with Carol setting up an assembly line down the long table where they did their orders. Adam had talked to his sister the evening before, and she promised that she and Tom would be there to help. By the time the others began arriving, the flowers had been unloaded and soaked in preservative.

Diane looked at the huge number of red and white carnations that had to be made into boutonnieres, and sighed.

"We're going to pull this off," Adam whispered, giving her a quick hug after she demonstrated how to trim the stem, insert the wire and wrap each flower with the florist's tape. "Is that the right length?" He was trimming flower stems.

"That's fine." Diane moved down the table, checking everyone's work. Next to Adam, Jim, Tom and Carol were inserting wire. Marilyn, Lori and Chris were wrapping the stems and Diane's mother stuck each completed boutonniere with a pearl-topped boutonniere pin. As the flowers were finished, they were put into the sectioned trays in groups of ten. After a very short time, Diane was surprised to see that the group was turning out boutonnieres at a respectable rate. It was frustrating that all she could do was supervise, but her wrist was almost too sore to bend despite the aspirin she had been taking. She knew if she abused it now, it would take even longer to heal.

When the others had the hang of it, Marilyn and Carol stopped to make up the special corsages for the bank employees.

"Those are pretty," Chris said.

"The employees would probably rather have a raise," Carol said, flashing Diane an impudent grin. "I would."

"If we pull this off, I'll have to think about it," Diane replied amid the chuckles. Business had been growing steadily.

The work went quickly, surrounded by much chatter and kidding. Music poured from the radio Jean had brought with her. After a couple of hours the crew took a break and ate the pizzas that Diane had ordered. Then they returned to work. Diane went into the rest room to comb her hair and splash water on her face. When she got back, Adam was supervising the stacking of the completed plastic trays into the cooler. The forty-degree temperature would preserve the carnations at their peak of maturity until next morning.

"How are we doing, boss?" His grin brought an answering smile to her stiff lips.

"Better than I had hoped," she said, looking around. "This was a good idea."

He leaned closer. "You can thank me later."

Diane felt the blush spreading across her cheeks. "We aren't done yet," she warned.

"Always so practical," Adam muttered before he went back to work. For a moment Diane watched him as he encouraged the others to finish the boxes of flowers that were left. It was frustrating for her to remain idle when everyone else was so busy.

"You and Adam make a pretty good team," her mother said on her way by to get more boutonniere pins.

"He's full of surprises," Diane said thoughtfully. They made a good team in more ways than one. She barely noticed when her mother went back to her place at the worktable. Diane was too busy dealing with the realization that Adam had infiltrated every corner of her life and heart, when he turned and saw her watching him.

He winked, and she felt a response begin to burn deep within her.

Oh, God help me, she thought, *I've fallen in love with him, and I never even saw it coming.*

9

"Is THE WAY we've stacked the trays okay?" Adam asked.

Diane blinked, focusing her attention on the glass cooler. "Perfect. Were you a florist in another life?"

He grinned and his brown eyes flashed. "Only if you worked for me," he murmured, tracing a line down her cheek.

Diane saw that her mother was watching them with interest. She smiled up at him. "Perhaps *you* worked for *me*."

"Perhaps," he drawled, "if the fringe benefits suited me."

Diane slapped at his arm and went around him. She was surprised to see that the level of carnations in the boxes was much lower and that there were few empty sectioned, precounted trays left. They were almost done.

"We're going to make it," she exclaimed, glancing at the clock. "This is wonderful."

There were several smiles. "This is kind of fun," Jean said.

Jim raised his brows. "Beats washing dinner dishes and bathing kids, anyway."

Diane joined in the general laughter. Finally, when the last carnation was cut, wired, taped and stuck with a long pin, then added to the last try, Adam set it in the cooler amid a round of applause. Then Carol and Marilyn began cleaning up.

Diane gave each one of the volunteers a hug and a heartfelt thank-you. "I couldn't have done it without all of you," she said.

"Just give us a call if you have another rush job," Jim joked. "We work cheap—pizza and beer is our price."

After everyone had filed out except Adam, Diane turned to him. "Tired?" she asked, "or would you like to come by for coffee?"

He studied her briefly. "Sounds good. I'll follow you."

"There's something I want to talk to you about," Diane said, turning out the lights. They went outside and she locked the front door. "It's been on my mind for quite a while. See you back at my place."

All the way over to her house, Adam wondered what it could be. Was she expanding the business? Had she decided he was too much of a distraction? He couldn't think what she was getting at, but he was glad when he finally pulled into her driveway behind her van.

"I realized something tonight," she said, setting two mugs of coffee onto her kitchen table.

Adam swallowed, suddenly nervous. "What?"

Diane sat across from him and sipped her coffee, her jewel-toned eyes serious. "I have to either expand and continue finding big jobs like the bank and that new French restaurant, or line up more steady customers and stay the size I am now."

Relief flooded through him. At least she hadn't said she didn't want to see him anymore. "What interests you the most?" he asked, watching her face.

"What do you mean?"

"I mean, do you want to expand or do you want to do the big accounts like tonight, or what? What do you like doing?"

Diane thought a moment, turning the coffee mug around and around on the table. "I like designing the best," she said finally. "Actually putting the displays together. And I enjoy consulting with the customers, helping them to plan what they want for things like the weddings."

Adam nodded. "What would it take for you to be able to concentrate on those things?"

"More steady customers."

"And how could you get them?"

Again Diane was silent, forehead furrowed. "One way would be to break into society."

His eyebrows rose.

"Not me, personally," she said, "but if I could get the business of the local first families, I think I would have it made."

"Have you tried?"

"Oh, have I ever. They all use Costain's Floral, and they have for years. I've sent flyers and I've tried to talk to several of the women who seem to be the leaders but with no luck. I've even sent complimentary bouquets on several of their birthdays."

"What happened then?"

"They sent thank-you notes." Her voice was dry.

Adam shrugged and drained his mug. "Well, sooner or later there'll be an opportunity to change things," he said, scraping his chair back. "And when it happens, I'm sure you'll be ready for it."

Diane watched as he came around the table and held out his arms. "Time for my personal reward," he said.

"Reward?" She stared at his hand.

"For suggesting the work party that saved your pretty butt."

She rose and stepped into his arms. "Oh, that," she murmured right before his lips covered hers.

THE NEXT MORNING Diane was up early. Adam opened one eye and watched her get out of bed and slip into her robe.

"What's doing?" he mumbled sleepily.

"I have to deliver the carnations to the bank before they open," she said. "I promised."

He muttered something that sounded like a complaint as he dragged himself to a sitting position. His wide chest was bare, the sheet draped modestly across his lap. Diane took the opportunity to study him from beneath lowered lashes. He was beautifully made, powerful yet sleek, strong but lean instead of bulky.

"Mmm," he murmured, standing unselfconsciously to bury his head into her shoulder. She let her hands drift down the elegant slope of his back to settle on the warm, satiny skin of his tight buttocks.

"Let's take a shower," he said, moving closer. "Maybe that will help me to wake up."

"I guarantee it," Diane said, lifting her head for his kiss.

By the time they'd washed, rinsed, caressed and dried each other, they were both achingly awake, and aroused.

"We could skip breakfast," Adam suggested as they walked back into the bedroom and he eyed the bed meaningfully. "That would give us some extra time."

"Breakfast is the most important meal of the day," Diane pointed out, giving him a quick kiss before she rewrapped the Ace bandage around her wrist. "Besides, it only takes me five minutes to eat."

Adam sighed, pulling her into his arms. "Then give me a proper kiss," he demanded arrogantly. "Better yet, an improper one. You can chew faster to make up time."

A short while later, Adam followed Diane to her shop where he helped her load the trays of carnations into the back of the van. Leaving his car there, he drove the van to the bank. Diane was eager to deliver the large order before anything else unforeseen could happen.

"I'll be glad when my wrist is healed," she grumbled. "I feel like an invalid."

Adam took one hand from the wheel and patted her thigh. "Relax and let me help you," he said. "I enjoy it."

After they'd delivered the trays of flowers they rode back to her shop, where Adam, who had been silent since they left the bank, picked up his car. "Sure you don't need me anymore?"

Diane bit back the reply that danced to her tongue, almost blurting out that she needed him more each day. "I can manage." She stretched to kiss his cheek. "Thanks."

"I'll call you later," he said absently. It was obvious he had something else on his mind, but there was no time now to ask about it.

Perhaps he was planning his next project, she thought as he drove away. She waved but he didn't notice.

As it turned out, she didn't see or hear from Adam for several days. The bank was happy with their flowers, and Georgia Morgan phoned to place a standing order for three bouquets each Monday to grace the lobby and the manager's office. Since she had to favor her wrist, everything Diane did the next week seemed to take twice as long. She missed the afternoons she and Adam had taken off to go driving or bike riding in the country. When the weather turned hotter she thought of the cool breeze by the river and the seclusion of one especially private shady spot they had claimed for their own.

Several times she reached for the phone, then she would remember that remote expression on Adam's face when he had promised to call, and her hand would falter. Instinct told her to be patient and wait. Even if she wasn't sure what she was waiting for.

"Phone for you," Marilyn told her on Thursday morning as Diane stood at the worktable designing corsages for a club installation that evening. She was learning to work almost one-handed, but she still had several arrangements to do, including two floor urns that would stand on each side of the podium.

"It's Adam," Marilyn whispered as Diane picked up the receiver.

"Can you be ready at six tomorrow evening?" he asked as soon as they had exchanged greetings.

"Ready for what?" She had been beginning to wonder if she was going to see him at all that weekend.

There was a pause, then he cleared his throat. "We'll go somewhere nice for dinner."

"Sounds good. Where did you have in mind?" Diane thought of the Italian place south of town that had been remodeled.

"Wait and see," Adam said mysteriously. "Okay? Could you wear that dark pink dress I like so much, and be ready at six? Please?"

His tone was more coaxing than demanding, and she felt a frisson of excitement ripple through her. What was going on?

"Sounds mysterious," she said. "I guess I could be ready then."

She heard him release a breath, almost as if he had been holding it. "Thanks. I don't think you'll regret this. I know I won't."

"Adam!" she wailed, "you're going to drive me crazy with curiosity. How about a hint?"

"Sorry, no can do." There was a laughter in his voice. "See you tomorrow."

She meant to protest again, genuinely puzzled at his secrecy, but before she could utter a word, he hung up. Clearly the only thing to do was to work hard and try not to think about him. Or how much she loved him.

ADAM REPLACED the receiver, rubbed his hands together and allowed himself a grin of anticipation. Everything was set. It was going to be a special evening. He was feeling good about himself and his life for the first time in a very long while, and he wanted to share that good feeling with Diane. Maybe he was making too much out of sharing his feelings with her, but he didn't want to just blurt out that he loved her. He wanted the whole evening to be perfect.

Adam took the broom and began to sweep the floor with energetic strokes, thinking about her as he did so. He realized that telling Diane how he felt was merely a first step, that in time there would be more steps to follow. Since the move from L.A. Adam had not let himself think too much about the future; now, however, the image of Diane in it with him was enough to make him smile.

Adam hadn't planned on seeing Diane until their date the next evening, but something drove him to stop at her florist shop during his lunch break that day on his way back to his own business. He hadn't seen her for days and he missed the sight and scent and feel of her. If he was lucky her shop would be deserted and he could steal a kiss to keep him going until that evening.

You besotted sap, he thought. He had been feeling extremely righteous about the week he'd put in, working hard and completing several more small projects. That very morning he had driven to a town thirty miles away to attend an auction, successfully bidding on a '53 Chevrolet chassis he intended to restore and sell.

If he didn't watch it, he told himself as he pulled into Diane's parking lot, work was going to become a real grind. Not as scary a thought as it had been only months before.

"Hi, Marilyn," he greeted the older woman as he swung through the front door. "Where's the boss lady?"

"Hi, yourself." Marilyn gave him a flirtatious grin. They had been teasing each other since they'd first met, keeping it up on the numerous occasions he'd stopped by the shop. "The boss isn't here. Won't I do?"

Adam hesitated, pretending to consider her as he circled, ogling her ample figure. "Naw," he said on an exaggerated sigh. "Diane would probably kill me and fire you. Where is she?"

"Delivering an order. But she left a note in case you called." Marilyn pulled a folded piece of paper from the pocket of her smock. "I guess she couldn't get hold of you by phone."

"I've been out." He reached for the note and read its brief message.

"This doesn't tell me much," he said with a frown. "She 'urgently' needs to talk to me. Do you know what about?"

Marilyn hesitated, then moved closer, though the showroom was empty except for the two of them. "I shouldn't spoil it."

Adam could see that she was dying to tell him. "Oh, come on," he coaxed her shamelessly. "I can act surprised when I finally connect with her. What's up?"

Marilyn leaned across the counter. "I wouldn't say, but it's such good news that I've been dying to tell someone who would understand the significance."

"So tell *me*," Adam said. "I'm not a patient man."

Marilyn looked him up and down. "I guessed that," she said, and winked.

Before Adam could again urge her to tell him, she resumed talking. "Did Diane ever say anything about breaking into the local society market?" she asked.

Adam nodded. "She said she's been trying, but hasn't had any luck."

"Well," Marilyn continued in a gossipy tone, "I never managed to get their business, either. They're a bunch of sheep, always buy from Costain's, all of them. They're in a rut."

Adam's impatience must have been beginning to show, because she rushed on. "Anyway, first thing this morning, Dr. Quigley's wife called. He's the dentist who has that gorgeous brick house at the top of Highline Drive. Have you seen it?"

"Yes, I have."

"He's made a fortune in local real estate and she's one of the leaders of that crowd. Well, it seems she'd had a tiff with Mr. Costain himself, and she needed flowers for a big dinner-dance tonight."

Adam felt a warm glow of happiness for Diane. "And Mrs. Society Matron wants to give our girl her business?" he asked.

"You guessed it. Diane headed out right after Mrs.
Quigley called to pick up more alstramaria, antheriums and some ginger that she begged from two of the
other local florists for the centerpieces. There'll be two
hundred guests at the country club."

Adam remembered some of the parties he'd been to
in L.A. before he'd left. Two hundred would be a cosy
group.

"So you'll have a busy afternoon," he said.

"And evening."

That stopped him dead. "Evening?"

Marilyn leaned closer. Her chatty tone was begin-
ning to annoy him. "Oh, yes. We've got the Cooper-
Chandler wedding first thing in the morning, too.
Things'll be hopping around here for a while."

Adam straightened, as his spirits sank lower than lily-
pad roots in a stagnant pool. "Diane's working late?"
he asked carefully.

Marilyn smiled. "Mmm-hmm. We both are, but
don't think I mind, cuz I don't. My husband's going to
his lodge tonight and eating dinner there. I would have
been at loose ends."

Adam recalled the excitement in Diane's voice when
she had accepted his invitation. He had thought she'd
changed, but she sure as hell reverted back to type when
there was money to be made.

"You sure this is what she wanted to tell me?" he
asked, keeping the smile on his face by a sheer effort of
will. No point in making Marilyn feel embarrassed at
being the bearer of bad tidings.

"I can't think what else it would be. Did you two have
plans for this evening?"

Adam thought about the reservations he'd made,
and about the feelings he had intended to share with

Diane when the mood was exactly right. "Nothing important." He stepped away from the counter, crushing Diane's note in the hand that hung at his side. Stuffing the wadded-up piece of paper into his pocket, he did his best to look impassive.

"You'll get hold of Diane then?" Marilyn asked, obviously concerned. Apparently his expression wasn't as blank as he had hoped.

"Yeah," he drawled, smiling again. "Don't worry, I won't spoil the surprise."

Marilyn relaxed. "Good. See you later."

As Adam turned away it was all he could do to keep from swearing out loud. He pushed open the door of the shop, resisting the urge to let it slam behind him, and stalked out to his car. Considering the condition of his temper, he drove away at a remarkably sane pace and managed to keep to the speed limit all the way to his garage.

Once there he allowed himself the dubious pleasure of kicking a few things before he picked up the phone, cancelling the reservations for that evening and then leaving a message with Johnny's mother. Then Adam found a piece of cardboard and a felt pen, and taped a terse sign to the front door. The news he had gotten from Marilyn was twisting in his gut. He could hardly make sense of it. There was no point in talking to Diane so she could tell him herself that she had once again put her business ahead of him as she had done too many times before. Maybe she had good reason but it was more than Adam could take. At the moment he didn't feel very sympathetic toward her emergencies.

The memory of the other dates she had broken got tangled up with the lies that Penny used to tell him and the promises she failed to keep. Perhaps he was incapable of seeing any woman clearly. One thing that was achingly clear to him though; he needed to do some serious thinking and sort a few things out.

DIANE WAS LATE getting back to work, and when she walked into Diane's Flowers, Marilyn grabbed her purse and rushed past her. "I'm meeting a friend for lunch," she said on her way by. "See you in an hour."

"Sorry I was late," Diane managed to say before Marilyn was out the front door and gone.

Diane looked over the phone messages and new orders, then went out the side door to unload the back of the van. By the time she'd unpacked the flowers for the special order, Carol arrived to work that afternoon. When Diane told her about the Quigley order, she was as pleased as if the business were her own.

"What a lucky break for us. But will we have time to do all this?" Carol glanced around at the flowers Diane was putting into preservative.

"Sure. Marilyn will be back soon. I figured that, at the most, if she and I stay an extra hour we'll be fine. I have a big date this evening, but I'll be able to finish the wedding arrangements in the morning. They don't have to be at the church until eleven." Diane glanced at the clock. "My only worry is getting hold of Adam. I just need to ask him to pick me up an hour later so I'm not cutting it too close."

She tried the phone again. "I wonder where he is," she mused aloud when she had listened to the same message on his recorder one more time and left her name yet again. "He didn't say anything about taking the day off."

She called his sister's house but there was no answer. Then she glanced at Carol, who shrugged and began clearing stems and leaves from the worktable. By the time Marilyn got back from lunch, Diane and Carol were both busy filling orders for the weekend. Marilyn loaded the van and left with the first batch of deliveries. While she was gone, Diane tried Adam's number again. It rang and rang.

"I can't imagine what's happened to him," she said to Marilyn as the two of them were finishing up the Quigley order. The shop had been closed for an hour and, without interruptions, the work had gone fast, even though Diane was favoring her wrist. "I guess I'll stop by there on the way home."

Marilyn glanced up. "He was here at lunchtime and I gave him your note. He said he'd get in touch with you."

Now Diane was really puzzled. He knew she needed to talk to him and he wasn't around. Why hadn't he called?

"Did he say where'd he be?"

Marilyn poked a fern into the vase she had filled with gladioli. "No, he didn't."

Diane was getting concerned. "Did he say anything that might give me a clue as to what's going on?"

Marilyn unrolled some violet ribbon and snipped the end. "No. He did say you had plans this evening, though."

Diane shrugged, sure that Marilyn wouldn't have told him they were working late. She knew that Diane wanted to share the news about the new account herself. "Well, I guess we'll sort this out somehow. I'll go by his shop on my way to the country club. Perhaps he left a note."

DIANE STARED at the neatly lettered sign. Of course anything that Adam printed would be neat; he'd had a lot of practice. It was a wonder that he had refrained from printing the words Gone Fishing in calligraphy.

She jiggled the front door again, but it was locked. Then she cupped her hands and peered in the window. There was no one inside. Adam's car was gone. If only there was some way to tell how long the sign had been up. She wasn't sure if it had been meant to explain his absence that day or if he'd just left early to get ready for the evening. But why hadn't he been there any of the times when she'd called?

Nothing made any sense. The only thing left to do was to go by the duplex and leave a note on her own door in case he showed up before she got home from delivering the Quigley flowers, then hope her lateness didn't disrupt whatever plans Adam had made. Sighing, Diane got back into the van and drove in the opposite direction from the country club. Going by her place first would take longer but she couldn't think what else to do.

Hours later Diane only knew that she was tired of waiting. The evening had crawled by with no word from Adam, and she had spent it pacing to the window and back, flipping through a magazine without really seeing the pages and condemning Adam to the far reaches of Hades if he didn't have one terrific excuse for this latest stunt.

When she had gotten home from the country club, she took a long hot shower and then spent more time on her hair and face than she usually did in a whole week, before slipping into the pink dress he had requested she wear. Her hair was long enough to put up now, and she'd pulled it off her neck with a jeweled banana clip and curled the ends. As seven o'clock came and went, then eight and nine, her pacing had disrupted the style, shorter strands beginning to work their way loose and hang down her neck. Her skirt was becoming creased from sitting down so often, and the makeup she had applied with such care was less than fresh. She had long ago nibbled the colored gloss off her lips, and if Adam didn't show up soon she would be starting on her nails next.

"Where is he?" she asked Punkin for the dozenth time. "Do you think something happened to him?"

The cat blinked and began to wash his paw, unconcerned.

"Why am I asking you?" Diane muttered. "You've made your feelings about Adam clear from the beginning."

She rose from the couch and peered out the front window. No cars in sight. She thought about calling the local hospital again, but the last time she had talked to the nurse in the emergency room she had promised to let Diane know if Adam or any unidentified man with dark hair was brought in. The police, too, had said they would call. Diane didn't know what else to do.

When the clock in her living room struck eleven, she realized that it was time to face the fact that Adam must really have left on some "fishing trip." But why? She remembered the goodbye bouquet he'd been ordering when they had first met. He had explained to her later that the relationship had been casual and the breakup mutual, but what if he had lied? What if this no-show was her "goodbye bouquet?" It would be a little silly for him to send flowers, considering her line of work.

Maybe Adam thought this would make a clean and final break. Maybe he had seen the way she was beginning to feel about him even before she had known herself, and he'd panicked. Maybe he was an unfeeling jerk, and she didn't know him at all.

What a great time to realize how much she cared, right before she got the gate. As usual, her timing was less than perfect. Tears welled into Diane's eyes as Punkin jumped up on her lap, startling her. As she began automatically to pat him, he purred and licked her hand.

"Don't be so happy about it," she grumbled.

Punkin's ears went back at her tone. After a moment he relaxed, the deep rumbling beginning again.

After a moment, Diane rose and dumped Punkin to the floor. "Oh, sorry," she said absently as he meowed a protest.

With little hope, she phoned Adam's apartment and then the shop one last time. The only response was his electronically reproduced voice inviting her to leave a message. Biting her tongue on the scathing retort that came to mind, she allowed herself the woefully inadequate satisfaction of banging the receiver down both times. Then she fed Punkin, locked the door and turned out the lights before retreating to her bedroom to undress and remove the smudged remains of makeup from her face. When she tried to find a relaxing position in her lonely bed, even Punkin's warm body curled behind her knees was little comfort.

The rest of the weekend went by with agonizing slowness for Diane. On Saturday morning she dragged herself from bed exhausted from her sleepless night. Pride kept her from calling Adam again before she went to the shop, where she finished the wedding flowers and delivered them herself, making her wrist ache. She did go by Adam's garage on her way back to Diane's Flowers, slowing enough to see that the sign was still on the front door and the place was still deserted.

"You look terrible!" Carol, who had come to work while Diane was out, exclaimed when she walked in.

"Thanks a lot." Diane was too tired to come up with a clever comeback.

Carol rushed over, putting an arm around her. "Is your wrist giving you trouble? You don't look like you've had a wink of sleep."

"My wrist is fine." There was no way Diane felt like talking about what was really bothering her. "I just had a restless night, but I'll be okay."

Before Carol could say anything more, Diane picked up the mail and shut herself in the office. She stayed in there until it was time for Carol to run the afternoon deliveries.

Sunday, Diane was unable to settle to anything, although she did clean her apartment. The laundry and grocery shopping were left for another day while she willed her telephone to ring. As the hours dragged by it remained stubbornly silent.

On Monday morning she woke with a headache that nagged her the whole time she was getting ready for work. She no longer expected Adam to call, but she was still angry enough to tear strips off him when she finally did see him. She hung on tight to that anger, knowing that beneath it lay unbearable pain.

On her lunch hour she drove to his shop, wondering if he was irresponsible enough to not be there on a workday.

AFTER HE'D TALKED to Tom, who had urged him not to jump to conclusions, Adam had spent a miserable weekend at another friend's mountain cabin. He had fished and thought, and done neither with any degree of success. When he got home the only thing he had worked out was that he owed Diane an apology for disappearing. Just because she had planned to cancel the date was no excuse for his own behavior. This was the second time he stood her up and she had a right to be annoyed. Still, knowing that he faced a very unpleasant conversation, he worked all morning without attempting to get hold of her.

At noon he was thinking about going over to see her when a bright red Fiero pulled into his parking lot and squealed to an abrupt stop. As Adam gazed out the window curiously, a familiar figure fairly bounced from the car, auburn curls flying.

Recognizing the sensational body and attractive face, he hurried outside.

"Sheila! What are you doing here?"

The woman who had been the recipient of his last "goodbye bouquet" gave him a blinding smile. Adam realized with a start that her beauty left him totally unaffected.

"I'm in town picking up a few things, so I stopped to say hi," Sheila said. "And I wanted to show you this." She held out her hand, on which rested a spectacular diamond solitaire that caught and reflected the sunlight.

Adam took hold of her fingers and admired the ring. "Is this from—" Memory failed him.

"Yes!" Sheila exclaimed. "It's from Jason. We're going to Reno this weekend to be married."

"That's terrific. When did he pop the question?" There was a new softness to Sheila's face, and her eyes sparkled with happiness. Was this what love was supposed to do?

"Oh, it was so romantic." Sheila sighed. "He took me to a wonderful place in San Francisco for dinner. Afterward we went dancing." She started to laugh. "Would you believe that when the waiter brought my Harvey Wallbanger, there was a ring in one of the ice cubes? It took me forever to spot the thing, while Jason was itching with impatience. I couldn't figure what was wrong with the poor man."

"Good thing you didn't swallow it," Adam said, sympathizing with the unknown Jason over his moments of agony.

Sheila clutched his arm. "When I did finally see it, I fished it out of the glass and he got down on one knee. It was the most romantic thing you've ever seen."

Privately Adam thought he could do better than that if he ever put his mind to it. The image of Diane's surprise if he did made him smile. "So, where are you going to live after you're married?" he asked Sheila.

As she began to describe the house Jason was building, Adam's attention wandered once more to Diane as he indulged his fantasies.

"No point in asking if you're happy," he said to Sheila a few moments later when she finally wound down in her praise of her husband-to-be. Adam held out his arms to give her a congratulatory hug, knowing he needed to straighten out a few things with the woman *he* loved. "Good for you," he said as Sheila's heavy perfume threatened to choke him. "I'm glad you came by."

DIANE SLOWED DOWN as she got to Adam's garage. There was an unfamiliar sports car out front and beside it stood the man she had come to see. As Diane stared, he pulled the beautiful redhead who was with

him into his arms. Shock smashed into Diane with all
the force of a runaway train. Praying that Adam
wouldn't lift his head and recognize the Volkswagen she
had borrowed from Carol, Diane forced herself to
maintain an even speed as she crawled past, craning her
neck to look at the woman Adam was holding close to
his own rugged body.

From what Diane could tell, she was gorgeous. Her
figure in tight white jeans was perfect and her auburn
mane shimmered in the sun. Diane wouldn't have believe it if she hadn't seen them with her own eyes, but
now she knew with painful certainty why Adam hadn't
called. He had been otherwise occupied.

Sick at heart, Diane turned the corner at the end of
the block and pulled over to the curb, hands shaking.
For a long moment she took deep breaths and fought
the tears that flooded her eyes and threatened to spill
over. Finally she regained minimal control, blinking
away the unwanted moisture as she shifted and continued on down the street.

She was so pale and quiet that afternoon that Marilyn finally suggested she go home early. Too shell-
shocked to argue, Diane promised to have something
to eat and go to bed, even though she knew that what
ailed her wasn't going to respond to chicken soup and
bed rest. She had no idea what to take for a broken
heart.

By the time Diane got home the headache she'd had
that morning had returned with a vengeance, so she
slipped into her robe, took two aspirin and went to lie
down, certain she couldn't sleep a wink.

The doorbell woke her. The headache had gone but
she felt groggy from the unexpected nap. As she rose to
a sitting position and groaned at the dizziness that al-

most swamped her, the doorbell rang again. It was probably Marilyn coming by after work to see how she was doing.

"You didn't need to check on me," she said as she pulled her robe around her and opened the door. The last remnants of sleep were abruptly ripped away as she stared openmouthed at the tall figure who stood grimly before her, a frown marring his handsome features.

Adam!

10

ANGER AND HURT roared through Diane at the sight of Adam standing before her. She tried to slam the door but he was quicker, pushing it open with one powerful arm.

"I can tell you're glad to see me," he said sarcastically after he had forced his way in.

Diane folded her arms across her chest and glared as he shut the door behind him. "Do you blame me?" She was almost quaking with the turmoil of the emotions rushing through her.

Adam raked a hand through his hair. "No, I can't say that I do," he admitted, surprising her. "I came to apologize."

An image of the redhead she'd seen with him flashed before Diane's eyes. "Where's my bouquet?"

"What?" Adam thought he must have heard wrong. "What bouquet?"

Diane's eyes grew wider in her pale face. "Don't you usually hand out bouquets to your castoffs?" Her chin was angled defiantly but there was an underlying thread of pain in her voice. Did she perhaps regret what she had done?

"I don't know what you're talking about," Adam said briskly, moving farther into the room. Punkin leapt from the couch and slunk down the hallway. Adam glanced up in time to see his plume of a tail disappearing through the doorway to the bedroom.

"I just bet you don't."

He looked puzzled at her hostile response. "I'm sorry I left without telling you," he said in a rush, as if determined to get the apology over with quickly. "Even if you were going to cancel, I shouldn't have done that."

"Cancel?" It was Diane's turn to be puzzled. "Whatever gave you that idea?" Was he trying to shift the blame onto her? He couldn't really think she'd let him get away with that.

Adam rubbed a hand across the back of his neck as if he were worn out as he glanced at the couch. Diane saw red at the thought of just how he might have gotten into that exhausted state—with the help of a certain redhead.

"Mind if I sit down? This sounds like it needs sorting out." Even his voice sounded weary.

Diane's gaze glided past the clean but faded jeans that hugged his thighs, noting his red T-shirt, the logo for a popular brand of car wax splashed across its broad front. As always, her body responded to the raw male attraction of his. Firmly dismissing the memory that taunted her, of bared chest and hair-dusted legs, she perched on the edge of a chair across from him. "Where did you get the idea that I was going to cancel?" she asked again.

His answer floored her. "From Marilyn."

Diane shot from the chair. "You're lying!" Did he really think he could get away with something so stupid? Marilyn might like him but she wouldn't condone such an outright falsehood.

"Am I?"

Diane crossed to the front window, then whirled around to pin him with a hard stare. "You're trying to cover up your own irresponsibility. That's despicable."

Adam uncoiled his length from the couch and crossed to where she stood, color darkening his lean cheeks. Before she could prevent herself from doing so, Diane took a hasty step backward, but Adam didn't stop until he was standing so close that she had to tilt her head back to look into his face. Anger radiated from him in waves, and his eyes glittered with suppressed rage.

"Despicable?" he echoed. "What about some of the things you've done to me? How do you think I've felt when you put every wilted posy that's come along ahead of me? Cancelling our plans with no more thought than you would give pulling weeds. That's hard on anyone's ego, lady."

"Me?" Diane screeched, then winced at the harsh sound and fought for control. "*You* forgot the concert. Talk about how to make a person feel important. I warned you that my business came first, and I've had to make some painful choices."

Adam snorted derisively.

"At least I told you up front," she continued, ignoring the rude interruption. "You knew what to expect. But you didn't tell me about your poor memory. *I* got surprised."

"So I'm human," Adam shouted. "So I forgot. I said I was sorry. And I apologized for taking off last weekend. I haven't heard you say *you* were sorry."

"Sorry for what?" As soon as she said the words, Diane wished she could take them back. She hadn't meant to sound so self-righteous. But clearly someone had misunderstood something.

"Sorry for being such a workaholic," he snapped. "Sorry for putting money ahead of people's feelings."

"Oh, am I supposed to apologize for being ambitious? It isn't a dirty word, you know. And I think it's better to have some goals than to drift aimlessly, to squander your talent like *you* do." Diane took a deep breath, prepared to go on.

"I can see there's no point in discussing this," Adam growled before she could say anything else. "If you come to your senses, you know where to find me." With that he turned and wrenched open the front door before Diane could collect her scattered wits.

"Don't hold your breath," she shouted after him as he went to his car. Part of her wanted to keep him from leaving, but somehow her lips and tongue wouldn't form the necessary words to ask him to stay.

The only indication that Adam had heard her parting shot was the chilling glance he bestowed on her before he hurled himself behind the wheel. His face had been frozen with cold fury, but for just a second Diane thought she had seen something else underlying the anger. Something more vulnerable.

Adam's temper carried him along until he was halfway home. Then he forced his fingers to relax their death grip on the steering wheel and backed off the accelerator, thankful that he hadn't crossed the path of a conscientious policeman before he'd realized how fast he was going.

What had happened to the laid-back, uninvolved attitude he had worked so hard on the last two years? All the emotional distance he'd decided was necessary to spare him from the kind of pain that desertion, by death or deliberate betrayal, could bring?

His mind and heart had finally convinced him that Diane was a woman he could love and did love, not when they'd been in bed together but, surprisingly enough, when they had been working on those damned carnation corsages. Her beauty, her spirit and the prickles in her personality had first attracted him. Her vulnerability and the honesty of her passionate response had kept him at her side despite the problems they faced. But the combination of mutual support, respect and need, and a closeness that Adam had never experienced before, was what had made him realize that he cared for her to a degree he hadn't thought existed. Her faith in him had made him feel invulnerable but only if she were at his side.

Now the words they had hurled at each other stained his earlier feelings. Not only had Diane been willing to break their date, she had called him a liar besides. Determined to find real changes in her character, Adam had allowed himself to believe that a few afternoons playing hooky symbolized an overhaul in her value department. First Penny and now Diane had turned out to be nothing as they seemed, and the pain slicing through Adam when he thought about Diane only emphasized beyond a doubt that his strongest emotion toward Penny had been guilt.

The path he'd chosen upon leaving L.A. had been the sensible one after all. It was safer and infinitely less painful to care little about anything, business or pleasure. Too bad Adam had jobs lined up for the next several weeks; he'd been turning back into an ambitious fool and now he'd have to pay for it by completing the projects he'd promised to do. It was small consolation that he would be kept too busy to think.

FOR THE NEXT two weeks, Diane threw herself into her work. She intentionally crammed every possible moment with designing arrangements, holding consultations, filling out paperwork, delivering flowers and doing so much at the shop that Carol and Marilyn had little to keep them occupied except to watch the human dynamo in action and worry about the emotional state that drove her.

Even though Diane kept a smile pinned on her face at all times she knew she wasn't fooling them. But as long as no one said anything to destroy her fragile disguise, she could pretend that everything was fine. Business was booming after her successful professional debut at Mrs. Quigley's dinner-dance. The society matron had not hesitated to recommend Diane to all her cronies, and several of them had already called the shop to order everything from table centerpieces to a funeral wreath for a beloved pet.

Perhaps in time Diane would be able to convince herself that running a successful business was enough to fill her mind and heart as she had once so passionately believed. Perhaps in time the sweet images of Adam and the hours they had spent together that flashed through her head like a colorful slide show would fade to the consistency of pleasant but unimportant memories.

"I'm leaving," Marilyn said, breaking into Diane's thoughts. "It's time to close up and you should go home, too."

"I have a few things to finish up," Diane responded, "have a nice evening."

"There's nothing left to do," Marilyn said as she dug in her purse for her car keys.

Diane glanced around absently. There must be some small chore that would postpone the inevitable return to her apartment. Even Punkin's companionship didn't cheer her as it once had. Now that she knew what had been missing from her life . . . Diane glanced up to see Marilyn staring with a worried expression on her lined face.

"I won't stay long," Diane promised.

The older woman let out a loud sigh. "Why don't you come home with me. I left a stew in the crockpot this morning, and there's plenty. We can eat and then you can go to bingo with Pete and me. It would do you good to get out."

Diane's smile became genuine. "Thanks for the offer," she said, "but I think I'll just head home. I guess I'm more tired than I thought." *And I'd be rotten company,* she added silently.

"You sure?" Concern etched deeper lines on Marilyn's comfortable features. She and Diane had become friends.

Diane shrugged. There was an ache between her shoulders that blended with the permanent ache in her heart. "I'm sure." She gave Marilyn's arm a reassuring pat. "Thanks for caring."

Marilyn wiped at her eyes. "Time does heal," she said after a moment.

Diane had confided that she was no longer seeing Adam, but Marilyn didn't know why and Diane knew she wouldn't ask.

"He used you in his lie," Diane said suddenly, not realizing that she was going to speak until the words left her mouth. "Adam claimed you'd told him I was going to break our date."

Marilyn frowned, obviously trying to make sense out of what Diane had told her. "I don't understand," she said finally. Then, as Diane watched, her eyes went wide and the color leached from her face. "Oh, my Lord," she muttered, stricken. "When did this happen?"

Diane stared, swallowing. "That Friday night, two weeks ago. It was when you and I stayed late to do the Quigley order. Adam and I had plans, but he went fishing instead and didn't show up until the following Monday. Then he had the nerve to accuse me of planning to cancel our date." Her anger and pain came flooding back, as raw as when they had confronted each other across her living room.

Marilyn looked away, twisting the straps of her purse with one arthritic hand. "This is awful," she whispered.

A feeling of nausea sluiced through Diane. "I don't understand."

"I told him that we were both working late." Marilyn's voice rose with agitation. "I knew you wanted to tell him about the Quigley job yourself, but I was so excited. He came in while you were gone and I gave him your note." The words were coming out in a rush, but not fast enough for Diane, whose throat had closed on sudden tension.

"He asked if I knew what the note was about," Marilyn continued, tired eyes pleading. "I couldn't help myself. Before I could stop I'd told him all about it, and I said we'd be working late. That night. He looked kind of funny then. I did ask if you and he had plans, but he said 'nothing important.'" Her fingers curled around Diane's wrist. "I'm so sorry," she said. "He said he would talk to you, and I never gave it another thought, except to feel guilty that I'd spilled your good news."

Diane sat down, suddenly as tired as if she had wired a hundred rose arches. Lord, what a mess. And it was partially her own fault; if she hadn't been reluctant to discuss the breakup it would have been sorted out much sooner.

"It's okay," she said. Then she remembered with painful clarity the dazzling redhead she'd seen wrapped in Adam's arms. "I don't think you caused anything that wasn't going to happen soon anyway. It just happened a little quicker, I guess."

Marilyn's forehead was wrinkled with concern. "I think you should talk to Adam, get it straightened out."

Diane remembered the way he had looked when he left her apartment. "There's no point. Believe me, there's no point at all." Adam hadn't trusted her and she couldn't trust him. Without it, they had nothing.

When Diane got home and unlocked the front door, Punkin pushed his flat face through the opening. Instead of greeting her with a series of meows as he usually did, he bolted past her to the relative freedom of the small square of lawn and narrow flower bed brimming with marigolds and petunias.

Diane wasn't concerned. Punkin occasionally went out for a stroll or some sun. He usually didn't stay long, jumping on the window box and calling through the glass when he was ready to come in.

That's probably what would have happened this time if a large black dog hadn't been loping up the street at the same time that Punkin was rolling on the warm cement of the sidewalk.

Punkin hated dogs.

The overweight cat and the canine with lolling tongue must have seen each other at about the same time. Diane reached to scoop up Punkin. The dog bounded toward them, barking. Punkin, as perverse was most cats, darted around Diane, saw that the front door was shut and made a sharp turn, dodging his owner's outstretched arms. He dashed across the driveway shared with Diane's unfriendly neighbors, the dog hot on his heels.

"No, Punkin, no!" she shouted when she saw where her cat was headed.

Punkin hit the base of Mr. Burn's walnut tree without slacking speed, running up its trunk as the dog sank to his haunches, barking even louder.

"Thanks a lot," Diane told the dog, who wagged his tail. She looked up at Punkin, his orange fur easy to see amid the tree's green leaves. He looked down and then climbed a couple of feet higher.

"Shoo!" Diane told the dog.

"Woof!" His mouth widened into a grin.

Feeling foolish, Diane waved her arms and clapped her hands, shouting. After a last look at the treed cat, the dog loped off, obviously disappointed that the game was over. Diane pushed her bangs back and reached for Punkin but the cat was too high. As she called his name and tried to coax him down, a sudden breeze shivered through the leaves. Punkin wobbled and then scrambled upward another three feet.

"Damn it!" Diane exclaimed. "I'm trying to help you."

He climbed onto a sturdy branch and, balancing carefully, pulled himself along its length facing away from the trunk. Then he stared down at her, tail twitching.

"Don't you dare blame me!" Diane exclaimed.

Determined, she called again, holding out her arms. "Here, kitty, kitty. Nice kitty, come on now."

For a moment it looked as if Punkin might try to work his way down to her. Hesitantly he stretched a front paw out to the branch below. His back foot slipped and he swung around, shinnying up the trunk a couple more feet until he again stopped to rest on another branch.

Just tilting her head back was giving Diane a headache, but the wind was coming up and Punkin again slipped a little as he repositioned himself. Diane tried to remember what she'd read about cats in trees. Leave them alone and they'll come down when they're hungry? Was that right? Could Punkin climb back down on his own? She called again. He tried to move closer and slipped again, scaring both of them as he grabbed wildly for a limb, wrapping his legs around it and meowing pitifully, ears flat to his head as Diane felt tears flood her eyes.

"Stay there! I'll get you down." She glanced around but there wasn't a soul in sight. Punkin meowed again, piteously. Diane couldn't bear it if he was hurt.

She circled the tree, wondering if she could climb it, but the limbs didn't look strong enough to support her weight. Besides, the lowest branches were still too tall for her to reach. She didn't own a ladder and she didn't know a neighbor who did. Cold sweat popped out on her chilled skin as she pictured herself climbing the good fifteen feet up to where Punkin perched, staring down and still meowing. Diane's mouth went dry and her hands clenched.

She knew with dreaded certainty that even if she had a ladder she would not be able to force herself to climb it, not even for her beloved kitty.

For a half hour she called and coaxed, but Punkin wouldn't budge. Then another gust of wind shook the branches and he howled again. Diane's heart stuck somewhere in her throat. She had to do something.

As she tried to think rationally, the sound of Adam's voice confidently telling her that he liked animals popped into her memory. He had no reason to like Punkin, but Adam wasn't the kind of person to withhold his help because of the way he felt about the cat. Or her, she hoped.

Above her head, Punkin cried again. This wasn't the time to let pride get in her way. "Hold on, baby, I'll be right back," she assured him before she raced inside.

There was no answer at Adam's apartment. Slamming down the receiver, she glanced at the clock. The lateness of the hour surprised her. He was probably out for the evening. Diane cut off her train of thought before it went any further. Still, fear for poor Punkin's fragile bones made her try once more. She dialed the number of the garage, even though she knew Adam wouldn't be working at this hour.

He answered on the second ring, and she could hear laughter in the background. Masculine laughter.

Relief threatened to swamp what little composure Diane had left. "It's me," she said, gulping back tears. Then her throat closed.

"Diane?" She could hear the surprise in Adam's voice.

"Yes," she croaked. "Are you busy?"

His tone became wary. "Well, I am talking to a potential customer about painting some company cars."

Terrific. "Oh," she said.

Punkin gave a terrified yowl.

"Just a minute!" Diane dropped the phone and raced outside, relieved to see the cat in the same place he'd been before. "Stay there," she ordered him before she ran back inside.

She could hear a tinny voice calling her name as she scooped up the receiver. Outside, Punkin meowed again.

"Adam, I need you!" Diane burst out. "I'm sorry to interrupt but—"

"What is it?" His voice turned urgent. "What's wrong?"

Without warning, Diane burst into tears.

"Diane, Diane, what's the matter?" he shouted.

"Punkin went up a tree," she began to explain, feeling more foolish by the moment. "I shouldn't have called but—"

His voice was blessedly firm and reassuring. "You did right to call me. I'll get a ladder."

"But, Adam, your meeting must be important." Guilt flooded through her. She should have called someone else, the fire department, one of her brothers-in-law. She hadn't thought.

"Go back outside," Adam's steady voice told her. "Do what you can to keep Punkin calm. As soon as I get the ladder I'll be there."

"Adam!" Her line went abruptly dead.

IT TOOK HIM less than five minutes to get Punkin down. He put the ladder he'd brought with him against the tree, told her to hold it steady and climbed, with the agility of a monkey, up to where Punkin, ears flat to his head, began to crawl farther along the flimsy branch.

Adam reached out and scooped the clawing, spitting animal against his chest. Then, balancing carefully, he made his way back down the ladder, holding the angry cat with one arm as he leaned forward and gripped the ladder with his other hand.

When he got close enough, he handed Punkin to Diane.

"Take him inside," Adam ordered.

"Are you coming, too?" She hated to think that he might just drive off.

"Sure, as soon as I put this ladder back in the truck."

Diane glanced away from his penetrating stare, only to gape at the red slashes on his bare forearm.

"Oh," she gasped.

Adam followed the direction of her gaze. "Don't worry about it. Take him inside," he repeated, "before he gets into more trouble."

Diane carried Punkin into the apartment, talking to him all the while. When she let him go, he ran for her bedroom and the safety of her closet.

"Ungrateful wretch," she muttered, looking down at the snag he'd pulled in her knit shirt.

"I'll say," Adam commented as he came in, holding out his arm. The scratches, blood beading along them, contrasted vividly with his tanned skin.

Diane burst into fresh tears.

"Hey, it's not a mortal wound," Adam tried to tease her. "But it stings like hell. Have you got any antiseptic?"

She brought the medicine and some bandages from the bathroom. After she'd cleaned and covered the wound, she tried to thank him.

He patted her hand. "Don't worry about it, okay?"

She shook her head, willing the flow of tears to stop. "It's not just that it's Punkin," she said, hiccupping. "But of course I'd be heartbroken if anything happened to him." She paused to blow her nose on the handkerchief Adam handed her. "Thank you." Looking down at the damp wad, she set it aside, taking a deep, shuddering breath.

"It's also that your dad gave him to you, isn't it?" Adam asked quietly. "That makes him even more special."

Diane's eyes widened. "Yes," she admitted. "How did you know?"

"You told me."

"I mean, how did you know that made him so precious?"

"Cuz I know how much your dad meant to you," he told her. "I could see it in those gorgeous violet eyes of yours when you talked about him."

Diane remained silent, thinking over what he'd said. Adam was right. Despite her insistence to the contrary, and all the resentment she'd managed to gather against him, she loved her father very much. He had given her a lot, including the self-confidence to start her own business, and to believe she could make it a success. He'd done that by always having time for her and by making her feel special.

Haltingly she told Adam what she'd just figured out. When she was done, he leaned forward to kiss her cheek.

"I know," he said quietly. "And I'm glad you finally realize it, too."

"I've been blaming him for a lot of things," she admitted, "without giving him credit for everything he did right."

Adam smiled, the light of something she couldn't name glowing in his eyes. Before he could say anything, Punkin jumped onto the couch, surprising them both. Cooing, Diane reached for him but he eluded her and walked calmly over to Adam. While she watched and Adam sat very still, Punkin reached out to lick his hand, one swipe with his pink tongue. The man and the cat exchanged a look of perfect understanding and then Punkin, with great dignity, jumped back down and went calmly into the kitchen.

"I don't believe it," Diane muttered.

"Maybe we'd best just accept it," Adam said, grinning.

"I guess you're right." Punkin was pretty smart for a cat. "Oh, my Lord," she exclaimed suddenly. "Your customer! Is he waiting for you? You have to get back. Don't let me keep you. I didn't mean to spoil a big sale."

Adam was shaking his head. "Don't worry about it. Dalton's wife has cats. When I told him what was going on, he agreed to come back tomorrow morning. I just hope you don't see my leaving him to rescue your cat another sign of my irresponsibility," he added dryly.

His expression was teasing, but Diane recognized the barb behind it and flushed. "There's more to life than just business," she said in a subdued voice. "Besides, I'd have to be pretty ungrateful to criticize you for that."

"Does this mean you're ready to listen?" Adam asked.

Hope leapt high in Diane's chest. "I know you didn't lie," she had to admit, "and I deeply regret accusing you."

The expression on Adam's lean face was somber. "I leapt to a few conclusions of my own," he said. "What

I want to know now is just, what *were* you going to do that evening?"

Diane explained about wanting to ask him to come for her at seven instead of six. When she was done, Adam groaned and clapped a hand to his forehead.

"You mean we missed a whole weekend together because you wanted me to pick you up an hour later?"

Diane couldn't help but grin at his perplexed expression. "I'm afraid so."

"I misunderstood what Marilyn told me," he began.

"I know. She said today that she had spilled the beans about the Quigley account, but she hadn't realized it caused any problems between us."

"Actually, she wasn't the one who caused them," Adam said. "You and I managed to do that pretty much by ourselves, didn't we?"

Diane's head bobbed as he stood, towering over her. Then he reached down to grasp her wrists and gently pull her up with him.

"I feel like a fool," he said. "Jumping to conclusions the way I did. I've had the time to do a lot of thinking since the last time I was here."

Diane remembered the mysterious redhead. "You may not have been alone in drawing conclusions," she said slowly, knowing she had to clear the air about that, too. Staring at the neck of his shirt, she told him what she had seen.

Adam listened to her, frowning, then when Diane mentioned red hair his furrowed brow cleared abruptly and he chuckled.

"You remember that goodbye bouquet I ordered from you?" he asked.

"Ye-es," Diane answered hesitantly.

"I told you then that it was a casual relationship. Sheila was the woman you saw the other day. And you saw me hugging her because she'd just showed me her ninety-carat engagement ring and announced that she's getting married shortly. The flowers I had you send in the first place were congratulations for finding someone she could love."

For a moment Diane was quiet, absorbing everything he had told her. Adam must think her a prize idiot. "I've been a real dope," she confessed miserably.

"Yes, you have," he agreed cheerfully as her mouth dropped open. "And you weren't alone." Then he put his arms around her. "Are you free tomorrow night?"

"Why?"

"Because I think that two people who have been through as much together as we have, who care about each other as much as we do—"

Diane flushed and looked away, but he caught her chin and tipped it gently back until her eyes locked with his.

"—deserve another chance," he finished. "Don't you agree?"

She nodded, forgetting to breathe.

"Then would you please tell me that it would be okay for me to pick you up tomorrow night at six?"

Diane studied his face. She saw tension there as he waited for her answer.

"Okay," she said, bursts of happiness radiating through her, "but only if you promise not to leave me now."

Adam's eyes darkened and his smile faded as his hands slid up to frame her face. "That's a hell of an easy promise to make," he murmured, and then his mouth covered hers in a kiss full of passion long denied.

DIANE WAS LATE for work again the next morning, and not even the sight of Marilyn waiting in front of the locked door was enough to quell her good mood as she leapt from the van, brandishing the key.

"I was about to call you." At the sight of Diane's cheerful expression, some of Marilyn's worry faded.

"Sorry. We—I overslept." Diane felt her cheeks go pink. "I've been meaning to give you a key. Take this one when you do the deliveries and have a duplicate made." Diane unlocked the door and Marilyn followed her inside.

"Is everything okay?" Marilyn asked, concerned.

"Spectacular," Diane crowed as she raised the shades.

The older woman turned to stare. "Have you talked to Adam?" Her expression was hopeful.

"Well, let me put it this way," Diane said. "We started out by talking."

Marilyn's face relaxed into a smile, and she made an okay sign with her thumb and finger before ducking into the office to leave her purse and put on a uniform smock.

Later that morning Marilyn took a mysterious order to turn one of the rooms at The Swan Bed and Breakfast Inn at the edge of town into a floral bower. When Diane asked about it, she insisted that she knew the party was good for the bill.

"I guess I can leave a little early and decorate it on the way home," Diane said, glancing at Marilyn. "I can't be late tonight, but it won't take that long to set up some baskets and scatter rose petals across the bed." She hesitated. "You're sure about the rose petals?"

Marilyn nodded.

"And the baskets? Four baskets of roses and mixed flowers?"

Marilyn nodded again, face carefully blank. "Mmm-hmm. And a daisy chain on the pillows."

Diane snorted. "They'll wilt pretty quick without water."

Marilyn shrugged, then began to look at the day's orders.

"Well, someone's sure got romantic notions," Diane said, half to herself.

SHE WAS CERTAIN the day had been the longest she'd ever lived through as she finally left the shop with her load of flowers for The Swan, thinking ahead to the dress she would wear for Adam that evening, and wondering where they were going. She glanced down at her wrinkled shorts and white blouse with the smudges down the front. At least she had plenty of time to freshen up.

She had just finished arranging the flower baskets and was scattering rose petals on the bed as instructed when she heard someone coming down the hall. Tossing the last handful of petals, she glanced around.

"Adam!" What was he doing there?

"Hi," he said, coming into the room.

"How did you know I'd be here?" Diane asked, positioning the daisy chain so it draped attractively across both pillows. "Oh, I bet you saw the van parked outside. Were you on your way home?"

Without giving him time to answer, she turned and brushed off her hands, wishing he hadn't seen her looking so grubby. "I won't be late," she promised. "I'm done right now and as long as you aren't planning to distract me, I'm leaving."

He still didn't say anything. Diane noticed he was wearing slacks and a clean sport shirt. His hair was combed and he looked freshly shaved. She could smell the light musky aroma of his cologne. In one out-stretched hand he held a single daisy.

"I've been wanting to ask where you get these," Diane said, taking the flower. "Not from the competition, I hope."

Adam shook his head. "From the field behind my house."

"Oh. Thank you."

He just smiled.

"Oh, how was your meeting?" she remembered to ask. "Did you get the job?"

"Yeah, I did." He crossed to the bed and picked up the daisy chain.

Before she could tell him to leave it there, he stepped closer and dropped it over her head. "Pretty," he said.

Diane's fingers reached up to feel the chain. "Adam, we have to get out of here. You shouldn't be touching things."

"Stay right there," he said. "Okay?" He waited until she agreed, then he went back out the door, returning seconds later with a wicker picnic hamper in one hand and a tote bag in the other. While Diane watched, speechless, he locked the door from the inside.

"Adam!" she exclaimed, "we can't do this. I have no idea when the people who rented this room are coming."

He dropped his burdens on the foot of the bed and put his hands on his hips. Then his gaze raked over her, leaving a fiery trail. It was all Diane could do to stand still. Her lips burned to touch his and her body ached to feel his heat.

Not taking his eyes off her, Adam came closer, reaching to take her hands in his. "Diane," he asked in a deep, serious voice, "do you trust me?"

She answered without hesitation, wishing that she had trusted him sooner. "Of course."

He let go of her hands and bent down to unzip the tote bag. As she watched he withdrew an ivory nightgown trimmed in lace.

"I think that everything you need is in here."

"I don't understand." Diane looked from the swath of pale silk to the hunger burning in Adam's dark eyes.

"*I* rented the room. For us. Now do you understand?"

With a little cry, Diane threw her arms around his neck. "What a wonderful idea," she said, lifting her face to his.

A crooked grin pulled at Adam's mouth right before it closed over hers in a hungry kiss. The moment he felt her respond to him he plunged his tongue deep, savoring her honeyed taste. A shiver rippled through Diane as her head tipped back and she curled her tongue around his.

Without breaking the heated kiss, Adam swept her into his arms, holding her against his heart, which had gone wild. Her hands dived into his hair and she held his head still as she returned the kiss, her soft, seeking lips making him groan as the blood raced through him to settle heavily in his groin.

At last they had to break for air. Keeping her arms around his neck, Diane glanced down at the daisy chain, crushed between them. With a reluctant sigh, Adam let her slide down his body until her feet touched the floor.

"Why don't you freshen up, shower if you like, while I set out our picnic supper," he suggested, voice thick with passion.

Diane leaned close to bury her nose at his throat. "Mmm," she said appreciatively. "I don't know if I can stand to be away from you for that long."

Adam made a low sound in his throat. "I gave you a chance," he said, reaching for the buttons of his shirt.

They showered together, touching and caressing each other's bodies with meticulous thoroughness. Then Adam slid his big hands down Diane's hips to the curves of her buttocks, lifting her against him as she wrapped her legs around his waist. Bracing her against the shower wall, he slid inside. The warm water rained down softly as Diane threw her head back, adjusting to the feel of him buried within her. She had missed him so much! Her body, hungry for his, began to quiver around him before he even moved.

Feeling her response, he began slowly to withdraw, then surge forward. After only a moment her passionate cry stripped his control. With a hoarse cry of his own, Adam buried himself deep and joined her in explosive fulfillment.

After he'd regained his breath, he lowered her gently, then stepped from the shower and wrapped her in one of the generous bath sheets stacked on the counter. Pulling the other one around himself, he went into the bedroom and got the tote bag, which he set inside the bathroom.

"Don't be long," he said, dropping another kiss onto her swollen lips. "Dinner waits."

When they finished the gourmet picnic he'd brought with him, he in his slacks, shirt hanging open, Diane in the ivory gown he'd brought for her and the slightly crushed daisy chain, Adam repacked the picnic container. Then he scooped her up and tossed her gently onto the antique bed, amid the rose petals.

Turning away, he took a long-stemmed bud from one of the baskets as she pulled herself to a sitting position. He turned back to Diane and offered her the rose, as perfect a flower as any she had ever seen. Smiling, Diane leaned forward to inhale its scent and to better appreciate the beauty of its burgundy petals. As Adam let go of the stem and sat on the bed next to her, something bumped lightly against Diane's fingers.

She froze, staring at the object that glittered back at her from the rose's stem. Glancing at Adam, whose face had taken on a painfully serious expression, she slid the ring from around the rose and bent closer to examine it. It was gold, in the shape of a daisy with a diamond at its center.

"Adam!" she exclaimed. "This is beautiful."

"There's an inscription inside," he said, voice thick with tension.

Diane examined the band. "Daisies Do Tell," she read slowly. "A loves D forever."

Tears welled into her eyes as she laid the ring in the palm of her hand.

"Will you wear it?" he asked. "I love you so much. Will you marry me?"

Like a thirsty flower, Diane absorbed the love she could see on his face. "I'd be proud to wear it," she said softly, her heart overflowing with tenderness.

He took the ring. "When I saw how much you'd changed, I knew I could change, too," he told her. "I could put the guilt behind me, and the loneliness. I could let Penny go."

"You've taught me so much about life and love, and about trust. I'll keep changing," Diane promised.

Adam slipped the ring onto her finger, then stilled her lips with a kiss. "Shh. I don't want you to change any more. If you did you wouldn't be the Diane I fell in love with." He bent his head, touching his lips to her knuckles. "Your drive and ambition are part of the reasons I love you so much. If you didn't care so passionately and reach so high, you wouldn't be my Diane."

"And I *am* your Diane," she said, holding her hand to admire the ring. "I love you."

For a moment Adam stared down at her, all that he was feeling plain to see on his face. "I love you, too."

"You can have me, and your business, too," he added. "We'll complement each other's strengths and temper the weaknesses. I'll make sure you take the time to play, and you keep me on the right track, okay? We'll share our dreams."

Diane smiled, her tears brimming over. "You'll always come first in my life," she promised passionately.

Adam leaned closer to kiss her again. "And you in mine. And I'll keep bringing you daisies." His hand ran down the side of her throat, lingering as it caressed a rounded breast through the sheer silk. Her breath caught as his eyes darkened to black and stark need drew his features taut. "I want a short engagement," he rasped. "Okay with you?"

Diane smiled. "Okay. And then you and I will be together forever." She lifted her mouth to his.

Adam's eyes locked with hers. "Forever," he echoed against her lips. "And beyond."

HARLEQUIN

Romance

**This September, travel to England
with Harlequin Romance
FIRST CLASS title #3149,
ROSES HAVE THORNS
by Betty Neels**

It was Radolf Nauta's fault that Sarah lost her job at the hospital and was forced to look elsewhere for a living. So she wasn't
particulary pleased to meet him again in a totally different envi-
ronment. Not that he seemed disposed to be gracious to her:
arrogant, opinionated and entirely too sure of himself, Radolf
was just the sort of man Sarah disliked most. And yet, the
more she saw of him, the more she found herself wondering
what he really thought about her—which was stupid, because
he was the last man on earth she could ever love....

MILLION DOLLAR JACKPOT
SWEEPSTAKES RULES & REGULATIONS
NO PURCHASE NECESSARY TO ENTER OR RECEIVE A PRIZE

1. Alternate means of entry: Print your name and address on a 3″ ×5″ piece of plain paper and send to the appropriate address below.

In the U.S.	In Canada
MILLION DOLLAR JACKPOT	MILLION DOLLAR JACKPOT
P.O. Box 1867	P.O. Box 669
3010 Walden Avenue	Fort Erie, Ontario
Buffalo, NY 14269-1867	L2A 5X3

2. To enter the Sweepstakes and join the Reader Service, check off the "YES" box on your Sweepstakes Entry Form and return. If you do not wish to join the Reader Service but wish to enter the Sweepstakes only, check off the "NO" box on your Sweepstakes Entry Form. To qualify for the Extra Bonus prize, scratch off the silver on your Lucky Keys. If the registration numbers match, you are eligible for the Extra Bonus Prize offering. Incomplete entries are ineligible. Torstar Corp. and its affiliates are not responsible for mutilated or unreadable entries or inadvertent printing errors. Mechanically reproduced entries are null and void.

3. Whether you take advantage of this offer or not, on or about April 30, 1992, at the offices of D.L. Blair, Inc., Blair, NE, your sweepstakes numbers will be compared against the list of winning numbers generated at random by the computer. However, prizes will only be awarded to individuals who have entered the Sweepstakes. In the event that all prizes are not claimed, a random drawing will be held from all qualified entries received from March 30, 1990 to March 31, 1992, to award all unclaimed prizes. All cash prizes (Grand to Sixth) will be mailed to winners and are payable by check in U.S. funds. Seventh Prize will be shipped to winners via third-class mail. These prizes are in addition to any free, surprise or mystery gifts that might be offered. Versions of this Sweepstakes with different prizes of approximate equal value may appear at retail outlets or in other mailings by Torstar Corp. and its affiliates.

4. PRIZES: (1) *Grand Prize $1,000,000.00 Annuity; (1) First Prize $25,000.00; (1) Second Prize $10,000.00; (5) Third Prize $5,000.00; (10) Fourth Prize $1,000.00; (100) Fifth Prize $250.00; (2,500) Sixth Prize $10.00; (6,000) **Seventh Prize $12.95 ARV.

   *This presentation offers a Grand Prize of a $1,000,000.00 annuity. Winner will receive $33,333.33 a year for 30 years without interest totalling $1,000,000.00.

   **Seventh Prize: A fully illustrated hardcover book, published by Torstar Corp. Approximate Retail Value of the book is $12.95.

   Entrants may cancel the Reader Service at any time without cost or obligation (see details in Center Insert Card).

5. Extra Bonus! This presentation offers an Extra Bonus Prize valued at $33,000.00 to be awarded in a random drawing from all qualified entries received by March 31, 1992. No purchase necessary to enter or receive a prize. To qualify, see instructions in Center Insert Card. Winner will have the choice of any of the merchandise offered or a $33,000.00 check payable in U.S. funds. All other published rules and regulations apply.

6. This Sweepstakes is being conducted under the supervision of D.L. Blair, Inc. By entering the Sweepstakes, each entrant accepts and agrees to be bound by these rules and the decisions of the judges, which shall be final and binding. Odds of winning the random drawing are dependent upon the number of entries received. Taxes, if any, are the sole responsibility of the winners. Prizes are nontransferable. All entries must be received at the address on the detachable Business Reply Card and must be postmarked no later than 12:00 MIDNIGHT on March 31, 1992. The drawing for all unclaimed Sweepstakes prizes and for the Extra Bonus Prize will take place on May 30, 1992, at 12:00 NOON at the offices of D.L. Blair, Inc., Blair, NE.

7. This offer is open to residents of the U.S., United Kingdom, France and Canada, 18 years or older, except employees and immediate family members of Torstar Corp., its affiliates, subsidiaries and all other agencies, entities and persons connected with the use, marketing or conduct of this Sweepstakes. All Federal, State, Provincial, Municipal and local laws apply. Void wherever prohibited or restricted by law. Any litigation within the Province of Quebec respecting the conduct and awarding of a prize in this publicity contest must be submitted to the Régie des Loteries et Courses du Québec.

8. Winners will be notified by mail and may be required to execute an affidavit of eligibility and release, which must be returned within 14 days after notification or an alternate winner may be selected. Canadian winners will be required to correctly answer an arithmetical, skill-testing question administered by mail, which must be returned within a limited time. Winners consent to the use of their name, photograph and/or likeness for advertising and publicity in conjunction with this and similar promotions without additional compensation.

9. For a list of our major prize winners, send a stamped, self-addressed envelope to: MILLION DOLLAR WINNERS LIST, P.O. Box 4510, Blair, NE 68009. Winners Lists will be supplied after the May 30, 1992 drawing date.

Offer limited to one per household.

LTY-H891

Coming Soon

Fashion A Whole New You
in classic romantic style
with a trip for two to Paris
via American Airlines®, a
brand-new Mercury Sable
LS and a $2,000 Fashion
Allowance.

Plus, romantic free gifts* are yours to
Fashion A Whole New You.

From September through November, you can take part in
this exciting opportunity from Harlequin.

Watch for details in September.

* with proofs-of-purchase, plus postage and handling

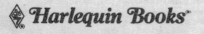 *Harlequin Books*®